Nothing Had Changed.

He was still totally hooked on Gabrielle. Bad enough before when she and Kevin had been engaged. But now one glance at her made memories of his dying friend roil in his gut.

Hank needed to check on Gabrielle as he'd promised Kevin he would, pass along his friend's final words, then punch out of her life for good.

"Hank, what are you doing here?" Her emerald-green eyes went wide.

Again he felt an all-too-familiar snap of awareness. It happened every time she crossed his path, the same draw that had tugged him the first time he'd seen her at a squadron formal.

One look at her then, in the ice-blue dress, and every cell in his body had shouted *mine.* Seconds later Kevin had joined them, introducing her as the love of his life. Still, right now, those cells in Hank kept on staking their claim.

"I'm here for you," he said.

Dear Reader,

I'm thrilled to have a book included in the Billionaires and Babies series! As a mother of four children well past their infancy, I found it a sentimental treat to revisit the precious baby years through a story.

This book also offers a double joy in that I found the perfect venue to feature a character readers have been asking about for years. The Landis-Renshaw family offspring have all had their stories told except for Major Hank Renshaw, Junior—son of General Hank Renshaw and stepson of Ginger Landis-Renshaw.

Many thanks to all of you who asked for this book. I read and treasure the opportunity to hear from readers!

Happy reading,

Catherine

Catherine Mann
P.O. Box 6065, Navarre, FL 32566
www.CatherineMann.com
Facebook: Catherine Mann (author)
Twitter: CatherineMann1

CATHERINE MANN

HONORABLE INTENTIONS

Recycling programs
for this product may
not exist in your area.

ISBN-13: 978-0-373-73164-0

HONORABLE INTENTIONS

Books by Catherine Mann

Harlequin Desire

Acquired: The CEO's Small-Town Bride #2090
Billionaire's Jet Set Babies #2115
Honorable Intentions #2151

Silhouette Desire

Baby, I'm Yours #1721
Under the Millionaire's Influence #1787
The Executive's Surprise Baby #1837
Rich Man's Fake Fiancée #1878
His Expectant Ex #1895
Propositioned Into a Foreign Affair #1941
Millionaire in Command #1969
Bossman's Baby Scandal #1988
The Tycoon Takes a Wife #2013
Winning It All #2031
   "Pregnant with the Playboy's Baby"
†*The Maverick Prince* #2047
†*His Thirty-Day Fiancée* #2061
†*His Heir, Her Honor* #2071

*The Landis Brothers
†Rich, Rugged & Royal

Other titles by this author available in ebook format.

CATHERINE MANN

USA TODAY bestselling author Catherine Mann lives on a sunny Florida beach with her flyboy husband and their four children. With more than forty books in print in over twenty countries, she has also celebrated wins for both a RITA® Award and a Booksellers' Best Award. Catherine enjoys chatting with readers online—thanks to the wonders of the internet, which allows her to network with her laptop by the water! Contact Catherine through her website, www.catherinemann.com, on Facebook as Catherine Mann (author), on Twitter as CatherineMann1, or reach her by snail mail at P.O. Box 6065, Navarre, FL 32566.

To Noah—may you always feel your father's love
and know that his memory lives on through you.

One

New Orleans, Louisiana: Mardi Gras

"*Laissez les bons temps rouler!*" Let the good times roll!

The cheer bounced around inside Hank Renshaw, Jr.'s, head as he pushed through the crowd lining the road to watch the Mardi Gras parade. His mood was anything but party-worthy.

He needed to deliver a message on behalf of his friend who'd been killed in action ten months ago. Tracking down his best bud's girlfriend added twenty-ton weights to Hank's already heavy soul.

Determination powered him forward, one step at a time, through the throng of partiers decked out in jester hats, masks and beads. Lampposts blazed through the dark. The parade inched past, a jazz band blasting a Louis

Armstrong number while necklaces, doubloons and even lacy panties rained over the mini-mob.

Not surprising to see underwear fly. In years past, he'd driven down from Bossier City to New Orleans for Mardi Gras festivities. This town partied through the weekend leading all the way into Fat Tuesday. If former experiences were anything to judge by, the night would only get rowdier as the alcohol flowed. Before long, folks would start asking for beads the traditional way.

By hiking up their shirts.

A grandma waved her hands in the air, keeping her blouse in place for now as she shouted at a float with a krewe king riding a mechanical alligator, "Throw me something, mister!"

"Laissez les bons temps rouler!" the king shouted back in thickly accented Cajun French.

Hank sidestepped around a glowing lamppost. He spoke French and Spanish fluently, passable German and a hint of Chamorro from the time his dad had been stationed in Guam. He'd always sworn he wouldn't follow in the old man's aviator footsteps. While his dad was a pilot, Hank was a navigator. But in the end, he'd even chosen the same aircraft his dad had—the B-52. He couldn't dodge the family legacy any more than his two sisters had. Renshaws joined the air force. Period. They'd served for generations, even though their cumulative investment portfolio now popped into the billions.

And he would give away every damn cent if he could bring back his friend.

Chest tight with grief, Hank looked up at the wrought-iron street number on the restaurant in front of him. Less than a block to go until he reached Gabrielle Ballard's garret apartment, which was located above an antiques shop. He plunged back into the kaleidoscope of Mardi Gras purple, gold and green.

And then, in the smallest shift of the crowd, he saw her in the hazy glow of a store's porch lights. Or rather, he saw her back as she made her way to her apartment. She didn't appear to be here for the parade. Just on her way home, walking ahead of him with a floral sling full of groceries and a canvas sack.

Hurrying to catch her, he didn't question how he'd identified her. He knew Gabrielle without even seeing her face. What a freaking sappy reality, but hell, the truth hurt. He recognized the elegant curve of her neck, the swish of her blond hair along her shoulders.

Even with a loose sweater hiding her body, there was no mistaking the glide of her long legs. The woman made denim look high-end. She had a Euro-chic style that hinted at her dual citizenship. Her U.S. Army father had married a German woman, then finished out his career at American bases overseas. Gabrielle had come to New Orleans for her graduate studies.

Yeah, he knew everything about Gabrielle Ballard, from her history to the curve of her hips. He'd wanted her every day for a torturous year before he and Kevin had shipped out. The only relief? Since she lived in South Louisiana, while he and his friend were stationed in Northern Louisiana, Gabrielle had only crossed his path a couple of times a month.

Regardless, the brotherhood code put a wall between him and Gabrielle that Hank couldn't scale. She was his best friend's fiancée, Kevin's girl. At least, she had been. Until Kevin died ten months ago. Two gunshots from a sniper at a checkpoint, and his friend was gone. That didn't make Gabrielle available, but it did make her Hank's obligation.

Gabrielle angled sideways, adjusting the sling holding her groceries and the canvas sack, to wedge through a cluster of college-aged students in front of the iron gate closing off the outdoor stairs to her apartment. A plastic cup in one guy's hand sloshed foamy beer down her arm. She jumped back sharply, slamming into another drunken reveler. Gabrielle stepped forward, only to have the guy with the cup block her path again. She held her floral sack closer, fear stamped on her face.

Instincts still honed from battle shifted into high gear, telling Hank things were escalating in a damn dangerous way. He scowled, shoving forward faster without taking his eyes off her for even a second. The street lamp spotlighted her, her golden hair a shining beacon in the chaos. She pressed herself into a garden nook, but the sidewalk was packed; the noise of the floats so intense that calls for help wouldn't be heard.

Hank closed the last two steps between him and the mess unfolding in front of him. He clamped his hand down firmly on the beer-swilling bastard's shoulder.

"Let the lady pass."

"What the hell?" The drunken jerk stumbled backward, bloodshot eyes unfocused.

Gabrielle's gaze zipped to Hank. She gasped. Her emerald-green eyes went wide with recognition as she stared at him. And yeah, he felt an all too familiar snap of awareness inside him every time she crossed his path, the same draw that had tugged him the first time he saw her at a squadron formal.

One look at her then, in the ice-blue dress, and every cell in his body had shouted, "Mine!" Seconds later, Kevin had joined them, introducing her as the love of his life. Still, those cells in Hank kept on staking their claim on her.

The guy shrugged off Hank's hand, alcohol all but oozing from his pores into the night air. "Mind your own business, pal."

"Afraid I can't do that." Hank slid his arm around Gabrielle's waist, steeling himself for the soft feel of her against his side. "She's with me, and it's time for you to find another spot to watch the parade."

The guy's eyes focused long enough to skim over Hank's leather flight jacket and apparently decide taking on a trained military guy might not be a wise move. He raised his hands, a glowing neon necklace peeking from the collar of his long-sleeved college tee. "Didn't know you had prior claim, Major. Sorry."

Major? God, it seemed as if yesterday he was a lieutenant, just joining a crew. Okay. He sure felt ancient these days even though he was only thirty-three. "No harm, no foul, as long as you walk away now."

"Can do." The guy nodded, turning back to his pals. "Let's bounce, dudes."

Hank watched until the crowd swallowed the drunken trio, his guard still high as he scanned the hyped-up masses.

"Hank?" Gabrielle called to him. "How did you find me?"

The sound of her voice speaking his name wrapped around him like a silken bond. Nothing had changed. He was still totally hooked on her. Bad enough before when she and Kevin had been engaged. But now, one glance at her made memories of his dying friend roil in his gut again.

He needed to check on Gabrielle as he'd promised Kevin he would, pass along his friend's final words, then punch out of her life for good.

"You still live at the same address. Finding you wasn't

detective work," he said, guiding her toward the iron gateway blocking her outside stairway. His eyes roved over the familiar little garden and wrought-iron table he'd seen for the first time when he'd driven down with Kevin two years ago. Determined to gain control of his feelings, he'd accompanied his bud on a weekend trip to the Big Easy. Pure torture from start to finish. "Let's go to your place so we can talk."

"What are you doing here? I didn't know you'd returned to the States." Her light German accent gave her an exotic appeal.

As if she needed anything else to knock him off balance. Good God, he was a thirty-three-year-old combat veteran, and she had him feeling like a high schooler who'd just seen the new hot chick in class.

He took in her glinting green eyes, her high cheekbones and delicate chin that gave her face a heartlike appearance. A green canvas purse hung from one shoulder, her floral shopping sack slung over her head, resting on her other hip. The strap stretched across her chest, between her breasts.

Breasts that were fuller than he remembered.

Better haul his eyes back upward, pronto. "I'm here for you."

The rest could wait until they got inside. He pulled her closer, her grocery sling shifting between them heavily. What the hell did she have in there?

He slipped a finger under the strap. "Let me carry that for you."

"No, thank you." She covered the sack protectively with both hands, curving around the smooth bulge.

Smooth? Maybe not groceries, after all. But what?

Her sack wriggled.

He looked at the bag again, realization blasting through

him. Holy crap. Not a satchel at all. He'd seen his sister Darcy wear one almost exactly like it when her son and daughter were newborns. No question, Gabrielle wore an infant sling.

And given the little foot kicking free, she had a baby on board.

As far back as she could remember, Gabrielle had dreamed of being a mom. Her baby dolls had always been the best dressed, well fed and healthiest in her neighborhood.

Little had she known then how very different her first real stint at motherhood would play out.

No daddy for her child.

A sick baby.

And now an unsettling blast from the past had arrived in the form of Hank Renshaw. Standing in front of her, tall and broad-shouldered, he blocked out the rest of the world. He wore his leather flight jacket in the unseasonably cool night, looking as tall, dark and studly as any movie poster hero.

She still couldn't believe he was here.

Hank.

No kidding, Major Hank Renshaw, Jr., stood on her street in the middle of Mardi Gras. Only her baby's doctor's appointment could have drawn her out into this chaos with her child. If he'd been a few minutes later, would she have missed him?

She hadn't seen him since… Her heart stumbled as surely as her feet moments earlier. She hadn't seen Hank since she'd said goodbye to Kevin the day they'd both deployed from their Louisiana base to the Middle East.

For some reason, he'd come to visit her now. And no matter how painful it was to think of how she should have been celebrating Kevin's homecoming, it wasn't Hank's fault. She was just tired and emotional. God, she hated feeling needy.

But oh, my, how the shower-fresh scent of him chased away the nauseating air of beer, sweat and memories. How easy it would be to lean into that strength and protection. How easy—and how very wrong. She had to hold strong. She'd fought long and hard to break free of her family's smothering protectiveness two years ago, following her dream to study in the States.

She was a twenty-six-year-old single mom who could and would take care of herself and her son. She didn't need the distraction or heartbreak of a man, especially not now.

Although from the horror on his face as he stared at her baby's foot sticking out of her sling, she shouldn't have any trouble sending Hank on his way quickly.

She plastered a smile on her weary face. "Oh, my God, Hank, I can't believe it's really you. Let's step inside out of this craziness so we can hear each other better. When did you get back from overseas? How long have you been here?"

"I got back to base yesterday," he answered carefully, his eyes shouting a question of his own, directed right at her son.

She ignored the obvious, best to discuss it away from here—and after she gathered her shaky composure. "Just yesterday? And you're already here? You must be more tired than I am."

Bracing her elbow, his hand warm and strong, he guided her through the throng. "Seeing *you* topped my list of priorities. Why else would I be here?"

Her son kicked her in the stomach, right over a churning well of nerves. "Well, it's Mardi Gras." She tucked her hand into the canvas diaper bag, fishing for her keys. "I thought maybe you came for the celebration, some R & R after your deployment."

"No rest or relaxation. My being here? *All* about you."

"About Kevin, you mean." Saying his name, even ten months after his death, hurt.

She saw an answering pain in Hank's eyes. What a strange bond they shared, connected by a dead man.

Turning away to hide the sheen of tears, she fit the key into the wrought-iron gate closing off the outside steps up to her attic apartment. The hinges creaked open. Hank blocked anyone else from entering and stepped into the narrow walkway with her. He closed the gate and turned fast, clasping her by the arms.

His steely blue eyes weren't going to be denied.

He tugged her son's booty-covered foot. "And since I'm here about Kevin, that begs the question, who's this? Are you babysitting for a neighbor?"

So much for buying time to pull herself together. "This is Max. He's mine." And he was sick, so very sick. She shivered in fear, her head pounding in time with the beat of the jazz band. "Any other questions will have to wait until we're upstairs away from the noise. I've had a long day, and I'm really tired."

In a flash, Hank tugged her diaper bag from her over-burdened shoulder. He shrugged out of his leather jacket and draped it around her before she could form the words *no, thanks.* She'd worn Kevin's leather jacket dozens of times. One coat should feel much like the other. But it didn't. Hank's darn near swallowed her whole, wrapping her in warmth and the scent of him.

Kevin and Hank may have crewed together on a B-52, but their temperaments were total opposites. Kevin had been all about laughter and fun, enticing her to step away

from her studies and experience life. Hank was more...
intense.

His steady steps echoed behind her as she climbed the
steps all the way to the third-floor apartment. After a long
day at the hospital facing her fears and making mammoth
decisions alone, the support felt good, too good. She fum-
bled with her keys again. Hank's jacket slid off and cool
night air breezed over her. He snagged the leather coat
before it hit the ground.

She pushed open the front door, toed off her shoes
and tossed her keys on the refinished tea cart against the
wall. The wide-open space stretched in front of her, with
high ceilings and wood floors, her shabby-chic decor pur-
chased off craigslist. She slept six steps up in a loft. The
nursery, tucked in a nook, sported the only new furniture, a rich mahogany crib covered by blue bedding with
clouds and airplanes.

Her studio apartment had been so perfect when she'd
launched her dream of coming to the States to pursue her
MBA. Since Max had been born, the place had become
increasingly impractical. She'd considered caving to her
parents' repeated requests to come home, but she'd held
strong. She had money saved and a decent income from
designing business websites.

Then the world had collapsed in on her. Her baby was
born needing surgery for a digestive birth defect—to
repair his pyloric valve.

"Gabrielle..." Hank's deep bass filled the cavernous
room, mixing with the reverb from the parade vibrating
the floor.

"Shh." She lifted her sleeping son from the sling and
settled him in his crib, patting his back until he relaxed
again.

One more swipe, and she smoothed Max's New Orleans Saints onesie. She cranked the airplane mobile to play a familiar sound over the noise from below. A familiar tune chimed from the mobile, "Catch a falling star and put it in your pocket."

A fierce protectiveness stung her veins, more powerful than anything she'd ever experienced before Max. She skimmed her fingers over his dusting of light brown hair and pressed a kiss to his forehead, breathing in the sweet perfume of baby shampoo and powder. She would do anything for her son.

Anything.

Weariness fell away, replaced by determination. She pulled the gauzy privacy curtain over the nook and faced Hank. "Now, we can talk. Max should sleep for another twenty minutes before he needs to eat."

Her son ate small amounts often because of the too-narrow opening from his stomach into his intestines. But hopefully the upcoming operation would fix that, enabling Max to thrive. If her frail baby survived the surgery.

Hank dropped the diaper bag on the scarred pine table near the efficiency kitchen and draped his jacket over a chair. "Is the kid Kevin's?"

His question caught her off guard, and she whipped around to face him. She'd expected anything but that. The doubt on his rugged face hurt her more than she wanted to admit.

Memories of happier times tormented her with how much she'd lost. The way they'd been coconspirators in reining in the more impulsive Kevin. How he'd helped Kevin rig a pool game so she would win—only to have her beat the socks off him all on her own the next round.

"Hank, you know me." Or she'd thought he did. "Do you really have to ask?"

"Between my sisters and my stepbrothers procreating like rabbits, I've burped a lot of babies. Your little guy looks like a newborn. It's twelve months since we shipped out." He shook his head, his knuckles turning white as he gripped the back of a chair. "The math doesn't work."

Her anger rose in spite of the fact he had a point about her son's small size. "Really? You think you know everything, don't you? Do you actually believe I would cheat on Kevin?"

Although hadn't she? If only in her thoughts.

"You wouldn't be the first woman to find somebody new once her guy shipped out."

"Well, I didn't." She crossed her arms tightly over her stomach. Her heart had been too confused to consider looking at another man. "Max is small because he has pyloric stenosis, a digestive disorder that has to be corrected by surgery."

Fear leached some of the starch from her spine. She sagged back against the corner hutch that held all her school supplies and books.

Anger faded from his face, his brow furrowing. Hank reached toward her, stopping just shy of cupping her face before his hand fell away. "Gabrielle, I'm so sorry. What can I do to help? Specialists? Money?"

She stopped him short, sympathy threatening to unravel her tenuous control. "I can handle Max's medical needs. I have insurance through the school. And you won't need your specialists to covertly check his age." Yes, she couldn't help but be suspicious of his offer. "His birth date is public record. He was born eight months after you and Kevin flew out. Max is four months old."

"So you were in your first trimester when he was killed. Did you not know about the baby when Kevin died?"

She swallowed hard. That, she couldn't deny. She'd lied through omission. "I knew."

"Why didn't you tell him before he died?"

How dare he stand there so handsome, self righteous and *alive?* She let her grief find an outlet in anger. "You two may have been friends, but my reasons are really none of your business."

His jaw flexed and he scrubbed a hand over his close-shorn hair. "You're right. They're not."

His nod of agreement deflated her anger. How could she explain when all of her reasons sounded silly to her own ears now? She'd been scared, and confused, delaying until it had been too late to tell Kevin. If he'd known, would he have been more careful? There was no way to answer that. She would have to live with that guilt for the rest of her life.

She tugged Hank's jacket from the chair and thrust it toward him. "You checked on me. Consider the friendship obligations complete. You should just go. It's late and you've got to be exhausted from your trip back. And honestly, I've had a long day with no time to eat."

A day full of stress on top of the exhaustion of feeding Max every two hours through the night.

She pushed the leather jacket against his chest. "It has been nice seeing you again. Good night."

He cupped a hand over hers. "I'm here to check on you, like I promised Kevin. And apparently my coming by was a good thing. Kevin would have provided for his child. He would want him to live in more than a one-room apartment."

Her head snapped back at the insult. "Back to the money again? I don't recall you being this rude before."

"And I don't remember you being this defensive."

Toe to toe, she stood him down. "I may not have the

Renshaw portfolio and political connections, but I work hard to provide for my son, and I happen to think I'm doing a damn fine job."

Her anger and frustration pumped adrenaline through her, her nerves tingling with a hyper-awareness of Hank until she realized… He still had his hand on top of hers. Skin to skin, his warmth seeped into the icy fear that had chilled her for so long she worried nothing would chase it away. Her exhausted body crackled with memories and heated with something she hadn't felt in a long, long time. Desire.

An answering flame heated in Hank's eyes a second before his expression went neutral. "Did you mean what you said about being hungry? Let me order us some dinner to make up for being rude."

"Dinner? With you?" She hadn't shared a meal with him since two days before he'd left for his deployment.

Since the night she'd kissed Hank Renshaw.

Two

Hank saw the memory of that one kiss reflected in Gabrielle's eyes. One moment of weakness that dogged him with guilt to this day.

She'd driven up to his base in Bossier City to say goodbye to Kevin before their deployment. The three of them had planned to go out to lunch together. But at the last minute, she had an argument with Kevin and he stood her up. Hank had bought her burgers and listened while she poured her heart out. He'd held strong until she started crying, then he'd hugged her and…

Damn it. He still didn't know who'd kissed whom first, but he blamed himself. Honor dictated he owed Kevin better this time.

Furrows trenched deeper into Gabrielle's forehead. "You plan to order dinner, in the middle of Mardi Gras?"

"Or we can leave and eat somewhere else. There's got to be a back entrance to this building." He kept talking to keep her from booting him out on his butt. "We can pack up the kid and go someplace quiet. It's not like he'll be able to sleep with all that Mardi Gras racket."

"This area's rarely quiet. He's used to it."

"Then, I'll order something in." He tossed his jacket back over the chair.

"Which brings us back to my original question. Who's going to deliver here? Now?"

He didn't bother answering the obvious.

She sighed. "Renshaw influence."

Influence? An understatement. But making use of it now was a rare perk in the weight of being a Renshaw.

"I guess even I would deliver a meal in this mayhem if someone paid me enough." She held up both hands fast. "But you're leaving."

He pulled out his iPhone as if she hadn't spoken. "What do you want to eat? Come on. I've been overseas eating crappy mess hall food and M.R.E.s for a year. Pick something fast and don't bother saying no. You're hungry. I'm hungry. Why argue?"

Hugging herself, she stared back at him, indecision shifting through her eyes. She was stubborn and determined, but then so was he. So he stood and waited her out.

Finally, she nodded, seeming to relax that steely spine at least a little. "Something simple, not spicy."

"No spices? In New Orleans."

She laughed and the sweet sound of it sliced right through him as it had before. He'd deluded himself into thinking his memory had exaggerated his reaction to her. And yet here he stood, totally hooked in by the sound of her laughter. Whatever she wanted, he would make it happen. He thumbed the number for a local French restaurant his stepmother frequented and rattled off his order from the five-star establishment. His dad's new wife brought hefty political weight to the family. And politicians needed privacy.

Order complete, he thumbed the phone off. "Done. They'll be downstairs in a half hour."

She placed her hands over his jacket on the chair, her fingers curling into the leather. "Thank you, this really is thoughtful."

"So I'm forgiven for my question about Max's father?" The answer was important. Too much so. Jazz music, cheers and air horns blared from below, filling the heavy silence.

"Forgiven." She nodded tightly, her fingers digging deeper into the coat. "You're a good man. I know that. You're just stubborn and a little pushy."

"I'm a lot pushy." The only way to forge his own path in a strong-willed family full of overachievers. "But you're hungry and tired, so let me take charge for a while."

"Look that good do I?" She rolled her eyes as she walked past him and dropped into an overstuffed chair.

Curled up with her long legs tucked under her, she looked…beautiful, vulnerable. He wanted to kiss her and wrap her in silk all at the same time, which she'd already made clear she didn't want from him.

So he would settle for getting her fed, and hopefully along the way, figure out why she had dark circles under her eyes that seemed deeper than from a lack of sleep. He crouched in front of her. "You look like a new mom who hasn't been getting much rest."

And she looked like a woman still in mourning.

Her eyes stayed on the nursery nook, the crib a shadowy outline behind the mosquito net privacy curtain. "He has to eat more often, smaller meals to keep down any food at all."

There was no missing the pain and fear in her voice. Right now it wasn't about him. Or even Kevin. It was about her kid. "When was the problem diagnosed?"

"At his six-week checkup we suspected something wasn't right." She adjusted a framed photo, the newborn kind of scrunch-faced kid with a blue stocking cap. "He wasn't gaining weight the way he should. By two months, the doctors knew for sure. Since then, it's been a balancing act, trying to get him stronger for surgery, but knowing he can only thrive so much without the operation."

With every word she said, he became more convinced driving here had been the right thing to do. She needed him.

"That has to be scary to face alone. Is your family flying out?"

"They came over when he was born. There's only so much time they can take off from work, especially since I live so far away." She set the photo down and crossed her arms again, closed up tight. "They offered to let me live at home, but I need to finish school. We're settled in a routine here with our doctors and my job."

"How do you hold down a job, go to school *and* take care of a baby?"

"I do web design for corporations—something I can do from home." She waved at the hutch in the corner. "Half my classes are online. Max spends very little time with a sitter, an older lady who works part-time at the antique store downstairs. She comes here to watch him when I'm away. I'm lucky."

Lucky? A single mom running herself into the ground to care for a sick child considered herself *lucky?* Or just so damn independent she refused to admit she was in over her head?

"What about *Kevin*'s family? Are they helping?"

Her chin thrust out. "They don't want anything to do with Max. They say he's too painful a reminder of their son."

Hank should have figured as much. The one time he'd met Kevin's family, they'd come across as self-absorbed, more into their vacation than their son. More likely they were ignoring Max because he interfered with their retirement plans. "At least Max has his father's life insurance money."

She stayed silent. Her fist unfurled to flick the gold fringe on a throw pillow.

Damn. He sat up straighter. "They did give him the money, right? Or at least some of it?"

"Kevin didn't know Max existed." She folded her hands carefully on her knees. "Kevin's parents were listed as his beneficiaries."

"I'll speak to them. And if they don't come through it shouldn't take much to contest—"

"My son and I are getting along fine," she interrupted. "We don't need their money."

Prideful? Needing to forge your own path? He understood that. Which made him the perfect person to help her. "You're doing an admirable job by yourself. I didn't mean to insinuate otherwise. I only meant that it can't be easy."

"That's an understatement." She smiled wryly.

"What about your parents?"

"Hello? I thought we already settled this. I'm fine."

"No one should have to carry a load like this by themselves. I recall from Kevin that your parents are good people." Although they lived an ocean away, in Germany.

"They are, and I did consider going home right after I found out I was pregnant. But I was already knee-deep in my graduate studies when I found out about Max. Sure, things are tight now, but I need to finish my degree, my best hope for providing a good future for my son."

"About those dark circles…?"

"I'll sleep after Max has his surgery because he won't be hungry all the time. He will feel happy, content…." Unshed tears glinted in her eyes. "I have to believe he'll be okay."

Her tears undid him now just as much as they had a year ago. He shifted from the sofa to crouch in front of her. He took her hands in his, her soft hands that had once tunneled into his hair, then down to score his back. Except now those nails were chewed with worry.

And he had to fix that. He couldn't let her go on this way alone with no one to help her. Staring at her bitten-off fingernails, he knew exactly what he had to do.

"That's the reason you're staying here rather than going to your parents, isn't it? Once you found out he was sick, moving to another country…"

"I couldn't start the medical process over again and waste precious weeks, days even. We're here, and we'll get through it."

He squeezed her hands. "But you don't have to go through it alone. I'm on leave for the next two weeks. I'll stay in New Orleans. I owe it to Kevin to be a stand-in father for Max."

A stand-in father?

Gabrielle froze inside. Outside. She couldn't move or speak. She'd barely gotten over the shock of Hank showing up here unannounced and now he'd said this? That he wanted to be some kind of replacement for Kevin with Max?

There had to be something else going on here. She'd heard of survivor's guilt. That wasn't healthy for him—or for her. "Hank, I don't know what you're trying to accomplish here. But Max already has a father, and he's dead."

His grip tightened around hers, almost painful. "Believe me, I know that better than anyone else." His throat moved in a slow swallow. "I was there."

Oh, my God. "When he died?"

"Yeah…." His grip loosened, his thumbs twitching along her palms.

His head dropped, and he looked down at their clasped hands, the strong column of his neck exposed. Her eyes held on the fade of his military cut. And strangely, she ached to touch him there, to stroke and comfort him. To hold on to him and let him hold on to her, too. They'd both suffered the loss of Kevin, and right now that pain linked them so tightly it brought the crippling ache rushing back full force.

Please, don't let her reach for him, which would have her crying all over his chest. The hint of tears a minute ago had brought him here in front of her…and when she'd cried before, they'd betrayed a man they both cared so much about.

So she gathered her emotions in tight and focused on him, and what he was saying.

"I tried to call you afterward from overseas, a couple of times, but calls out were few and far between."

"I got the messages," she whispered.

He looked up fast. "And you didn't write back? Email?"

His voice on those recordings had poured alcohol on her open grief. "It was too painful then." And his presence now? She didn't know what she was feeling. "I figured hearing my voice would hurt you as much as it hurt me to hear yours."

"Do you still feel that way?"

His deep blue eyes held hers, waiting, asking. She didn't have the answers and her life was scary enough just dealing with Max's surgery. She looked down at their joined hands and, holy crap, how long had they been holding each other like that?

She snatched her arms back, crossing them over her chest. "What are we doing here, Hank? Are you here to pick up where we left off after that kiss, now that Kevin's gone? Because you have to realize that was a mistake."

A dark eyebrow slashed upward. "If you have to ask that, you don't know me at all. I mean what I say. I just want to be here for Kevin's kid."

"But you didn't know about Max when you arrived." And why hadn't she thought of that until now? "What *are* you doing here?"

He shoved to his feet and paced in the space she'd decorated with such hope and plans, a blend of her dual roots. Then she'd met Kevin and thought, finally, she had found roots of her own, a sense of belonging.

Hank's powerful long legs ate up the one-room apartment quickly, back and forth in front of the nursery nook before pivoting hard to face her. "Kevin wanted me to deliver a message."

"A message?" A burn prickled along her skin until the roots of her hair tingled.

"I meant it when I said I was with him when he died." His body went taut, his shoulders bracing, broadening. "I was right beside him until the end."

She eased to her feet, steeling herself for whatever he had to share, for words that could haul her back into the agony she'd felt when Kevin died, when she'd given birth to their child alone. "What did he say?"

"He said he forgave us."

Three

Gabrielle looked every bit as stunned as he'd felt when Kevin said the words to him, that he forgave them. The memory blasted through him of that hellish night at the checkpoint when they'd been ambushed, the smell of gunfire and death. Then Kevin spoke and said the unthinkable.

That he knew Hank and Gabrielle had feelings for each other.

Her mouth opened and closed a couple of times, but no words came out. She pressed her palm to her lips, turning away.

He wanted to reach for her, to comfort her. Do something—since he couldn't seem to scrounge up the right words. He wasn't much of a warm and fuzzy guy. He was a man of action.

A squawk from behind him stopped him short.

"Max," Gabrielle gasped, rushing past him.

She swept aside the gauzy curtain and lifted her son out. Damn, the boy was so tiny. Scary small. The enormity of that little being going under the knife stole his breath and raised every protective instinct all at once.

Cradling Max to her shoulder, she patted his back. "I need to feed and change him."

"Yeah, okay. What do you need me to do to help? With all those nieces and nephews, I'm not totally inept."

"Unless you're lactating, I don't think you can help with this."

Lactating? Breast-feeding?

Ohhhh-kay. He grabbed his jacket off the back of the chair. "I'll wait downstairs for the delivery guy to bring supper."

She bounced the baby gently on her shoulder, his whimpers growing louder, more insistent. "The back entrance is just at the other end of the garden alleyway. Take the keys off the tea cart on your way out."

"Roger that. Wilco—" Will comply. "I'll be back in twenty minutes or so."

Pulling the door closed behind him, he stepped back into the waning Mardi Gras mayhem. The tail end of the parade blinked in the distance, the crowd following and dispersing. He scooped up a couple of strands of beads and a feathered mask that must have strayed over the gate. He wanted her out of here, somewhere safer. She had enough on her plate taking care of the little guy without worrying about someone scaling that fence one night.

He sidestepped the round iron table and chairs, decorated with a few potted plants and hanging ferns. Chick-pretty but not safe. He eyed the shadowy alleyway, not impressed with security. And he would damn well do something about it.

Reaching the back gate, he leaned against the brick wall to wait and fished out his phone. He thumbed through the directory until he landed on the name he needed. He hit Call. The youngest of his four stepbrothers worked renovations of historical landmark homes. Even a couple of foreign castles.

For right now, he would settle for something more local.

The ringing stopped.

"Hey there, stranger," his stepbrother Jonah Landis answered from on location at heaven only knew where. Jonah's projects spanned the globe. "Welcome home."

"Thanks, good to be back." Or rather it would be once he got some things straightened out. He needed to put to rest the feelings he had for Gabrielle and figure out a way out from under the guilt.

"How much longer until the base cuts you free for some vacation time?"

"Actually—" he crossed one loafer-clad foot over the other "—that's what I'm calling you about. I'm visiting a friend in New Orleans, and I'm hoping you can hook me up with a place to stay."

"What exactly are the parameters?"

Parameters? Privacy topped the list. His father was a retired general who'd been on the Joint Chiefs of Staff and now served as a freelance military correspondent for a major cable network. His stepmom—Ginger Landis Renshaw—was a former secretary of state, now an ambassador.

He hadn't grown up with that kind of influence. And even once his family stepped into the limelight, he'd lived a Spartan life, socking away most of his paychecks and investing well, very well. He could retire now, except that military calling to serve couldn't be denied. Even his family didn't know his full net worth. Only that his investments left him "comfortably" well off, enough to explain if he spent beyond a military paycheck.

Which he rarely did. But he needed something private. A place for Max to recover from his surgery, a place where Gabrielle would have help before she collapsed from trying to tackle everything on her own.

"Jonah, I seem to recall you were starting a renovation down here in New Orleans right before I deployed."

"Right, a historic mansion in the garden district that got whacked by a hurricane. It's an Italianate cast-iron galleried-style—"

"Right. I just need to know if it's finished and if it has a security system."

"Finished, security system installed last week, up for sale with bare bones furniture to help prospective buyers envision themselves living there."

Sounded perfect. "Think you can pull it off the market for a couple of weeks?"

"Any reason you're looking for a house rather than a hotel?"

"Hotels are noisy and nosey."

"Fair enough. What's mine is yours."

"I mean this as a business transaction. I insist on paying."

"Really, bro, we're good." Jonah paused for a second, the sound of sheets rustling and him speaking with his wife about going to the other room. "Seriously, though, why call me? Any of mom's or the general's people could have taken care of a low-profile place to stay."

Truth was easy this time. "Ginger would have heard about it, whether from her people or the general. She would have questions…."

"There's a woman involved." Jonah laughed softly.

No need denying that. And heaven forbid, he mention the baby and Grandma Ginger—his stepmom—would come running straight to New Orleans. "I want this to stay quiet for a while. The last thing I need is the press or our family breathing down my neck, not now."

"Understood." Of course he did. Jonah Landis's wife had royal ties as the illegitimate daughter of a deposed king. Privacy was a valuable commodity in short supply for them. "I can have the Realtor bring you the keys now."

"No need to disrupt anyone's Mardi Gras. I'll swing by tomorrow and get them myself."

"Party on, then."

"Thank you. I appreciate this."

"We're family, even if you hide out from the rest of us. Good to hear from you, bro."

And they were. Even if by marriage. His dad and his second wife, Ginger, had built something together after both of their spouses died. Hank looked up the iron stairs at the closed door leading to Gabrielle's apartment. She needed his help, just the way Ginger and Hank, Sr., had needed help with their kids. They'd turned to each other rather than go it alone. That's what friends did for each other.

Whether Gabrielle wanted his help or not, he was all in.

Gabrielle yanked her clothes off fast and tossed them all in the bathroom laundry hamper. Her knee bumped the sink. She bit back a curse, hopping around on one foot and trying not to fall into the tub in the closet-size bathroom. Any minute now, Hank could walk back up with supper and she needed to clean up after feeding Max. No bachelor was going to want to hear about—or smell—baby puke.

She didn't have time for a shower but at least she could splash some water on her face and change clothes. Not that she cared what she looked like around him. She was just excited over her first real meal with another adult since Max was born. Silly, selfish and she had to remember this wasn't a real dinner date.

Just supper with an old, uh, friend?

Oh, God, she was a mess. She sagged back against the sink. No amount of face washing or hair brushing was going to change the fact that she was a single mom, who wore nursing bras and eau de baby. Nothing was going to change that. She didn't want to *change* that, damn it.

Even if Kevin had somehow given her permission to fall for his best friend. The realization that he'd somehow known clawed at her already guilty conscience and made her feel like a huge fraud.

Frustrated and running out of time, she yanked on a pair of black stretch pants and tugged a long tank tee over her head. She grabbed a bottle of lavender spray she'd bought because it was supposed to be calming, soothing and she'd been searching for any help to relax her son.

Tonight, she needed some of that peace for herself. She spritzed her body fast, spraying an extra pump over her head and spinning to capture the drift. She scrubbed her hair back into a high ponytail just as she heard the front door open.

Time's up.

Her stomach knotted.

There was no more dodging Hank, that long-ago kiss and the fact that somehow Kevin had found out. She'd hurt the man she'd promised to love for the rest of her life. She rammed the lavender bottle into the medicine cabinet and padded back out into the living room barefoot.

And the breath left her body. Hank stood in the doorway, shadows across his face. In his flight jacket and khakis, he could have been any military guy coming home with supper for his family. Yet even with the anonymity of the shadowy light, she would never for a moment mistake him for anyone but himself.

The light clink of silverware across the room broke the spell, and she looked over to find a private waiter setting up things for them. Hank held out a chair for her at her little table that had been transformed with silver, china and a single rose. This was a world away from the sandwich and milk she'd planned for herself.

Their waiter popped a wine bottle—the label touting a Bordeaux from St. Emilion.

She covered her glass, even though her mouth watered. "No, thank you. I'm a nursing mom."

The waiter nodded and promptly switched to an exclusive bottled water as Hank took his seat across from her.

"Whatever that is smells amazing." She plastered on a smile as the waiter served their meal, then quietly left. "I concede you're the king of late-night takeout food. If that tastes even half as good as it smells, it'll be heavenly."

"So the little guy's down for the count?" His eyes heated over her, briefly but unmistakably lingering on her legs.

Was his head tipping to catch her scent? She had to be mistaken, sleep deprived and hallucinating. And if she wasn't, she needed to get her priorities in order. Max came first, and for him, she needed to eat and keep her strength up.

"Sorry about the wine but Max is nursing as well as bottle feeding." With his digestive problems, he fed more often than she could keep up with, even expressing. But that was far more detail than she wanted to share with him. "He will sleep for another hour and a half."

"You've got to be flat-out exhausted." He tipped back his water goblet.

"I'm not the only single mom on the planet." She set out silverware and napkins. "I'll survive."

And survive well with the meal in front of her. Aromas wafted upward to tempt her with hickory-roasted duck, cornbread pudding and on and on until her mouth watered. Reaching for the fork, she realized she was really hungry for the first time in months.

Sure, maybe she was avoiding talking for a few minutes longer, letting herself be *normal* for just a stolen pocket of time.

Until she couldn't avoid the burning question any longer....

Without looking up, she stabbed a fork into the corn bread pudding, mixing it with a roasted-corn salad. "What did you mean by saying Kevin had forgiven us?"

Hank set his fork down carefully on the gold ring edging the plate. "He didn't seem to know any details other than we had feelings for each other. He said he understood, and he wanted us both to go on with our lives."

Gasping in horror, she dropped her fork. Shame piled on top of the guilt. Kevin had known. Somehow he'd seen her confused feelings when she'd thought she'd hidden them so carefully. He'd been so argumentative just before leaving, picking fights with her about anything because she wouldn't agree to move closer. She'd held her temper in check because of his upcoming deployment—until nerves got the better of her.

He'd wanted her to skip out on work and party with him, but nerves were already chewing her over the last time he'd partied, gotten reckless and forgot birth control. She'd told him she was tired of always having to be the adult in their relationship. He'd snapped back, telling her to go hang out with Hank, then, since he was mature enough for ten people. The fight had been hurtful and a product of fears about him leaving.

How damn sad that a ridiculous fight led her to act on those feelings, to kiss Hank.

She flattened her shaking hands to the table. "Are you saying Kevin *gave* me to you in a dying declaration?"

"Not in so many words." He reached for his water glass. "He said he loved you, he forgave us both and then he mumbled something about being sorry for not taking you out for gumbo."

Tears welled fast and acidic. The enormity of what Hank had said, of his showing up here in the first place, exploded in her brain, then came back together like puzzle pieces fitting into an unsettling image. "You aren't actually expecting to pick up where we left off with that kiss, are you?" She pressed her fingers against her speeding heart. "Because that would be incredibly crass, if you came here looking for an easy pickup off your friend's death."

He choked on the water. "That *would* be crass."

"Glad we agree on that much. So why are you here again?"

"Gabrielle—" he set his glass down "—I'm here to tell you Kevin's last thought was of you, that he loved you and let you go. End of story. Or so I thought. But finding out Kevin had a kid? That changes everything."

Now he was sticking around because of Max? That should make her happy. Her son was everything, after all. Hank had said he wanted to be a stand-in dad. Yet something about the notion of him being here for her baby felt off. "Max doesn't have to change anything. You're free to go." She shoved her chair back sharply, just barely catching it before it tipped to the floor. "He is not your child, and he's not your responsibility."

Hank shot to his feet and grabbed her shoulders. "You know me better than that, Gabrielle. Do you honestly think I'm the kind of man who could walk away now?"

"You feel guilty." She gripped his polo shirt, the cotton warm from the heat of his body. "Even though he released you, you still feel bad about that kiss. Well, consider yourself absolved by me, too. I instigated it. My fault. Bye-bye."

She let go, pushed him away and raised her hands before she succumbed to the temptation to crawl right into his arms.

"Bull." He twined his fingers with hers. "What happened that night—it was me. I kissed you, and yeah, I still feel guilty as hell because if I had the chance, I would do it again."

Four

Hank stood so close to Gabrielle he could smell the lavender scent on her skin, on her hair. His body flamed to life, lust pounding through his veins leaving him hard and hungry. As much as he wanted to chalk it up to extended abstinence, he'd always felt this way around her. The day he'd met her, he'd been seeing someone else, a year-long relationship that he'd promptly ended. In fact, his abstinence stint had started that day, nearly two years ago.

Good God, much longer and he should get some kind of honorary monk status.

With Gabrielle this close, her hands linked with his, he remembered all the reasons he'd kissed her in the first place. Or rather *the* reason. He felt a crazy, inexplicable draw to this woman, a gut-deep need to claim her as his that wasn't dimming one damn bit with time.

Her lithe body was so close, motherhood having added some curves he ached to explore. She swayed, not much, but definitely toward him. Her sparkling green eyes went wide, her pupils dilating with unmistakable desire. Then she blinked fast, her shoulders rolling back. Slowly, she inched her hands from him.

"Hank," she whispered, her voice husky, accent thicker. "I think you should go now."

Disappointment whipped through him, quickly smothered by reason. Things were ten times more complicated than before and being with her had been damned convoluted then. He needed time to sort through the major bombshell the stork had dropped into his world tonight.

Hank stepped back, needing distance from her in more ways than one. He'd meant it when he said he would be here for her and her son during the surgery. He owed his friend—and he owed her.

The rest, he would figure out later, back at his place while soaking in his hot tub with a beer. "I'll be here at nine to take you to the baby's appointment."

She tugged at the collar of her loose tank top. "How did you know he has another appointment tomorrow?"

For a self-indulgent second, he let his eyes linger on the curve of her breasts under the silky cotton, her slim thighs hugged by black leggings. "You left the slip from the doctor's office under a magnet on the fridge. Some kind of early registration work at the hospital, right? He has surgery the day after tomorrow?"

"Yes to all, but Hank, this is my son, my life. I can handle it on my own."

"Yes, you can." And that was one of the things he admired about Gabrielle, her independence. God, he was so screwed. "But you don't have to."

The next morning, Gabrielle hitched the diaper bag over her shoulder, grabbing an extra receiving blanket at the last second. She was seriously scattered this morning. It was tough enough getting out the door with a baby, but leaving a half hour earlier than expected was darn near impossible.

Still, she was determined to go before Hank showed up. His sudden arrival last night, his words, his touch—just the sound of his voice—had tipped her world upside down. The twisted sheets and coverlet on her bed attested to how he'd plagued her dreams. First, he'd been wearing a mask, dark and mysterious with blues music and fog wrapping around him. Then she'd been the one in disguise, but her mask took on a more sensual tone, her clothes and inhibitions falling away....

Nerves tingling to the roots of her hair, she turned away from her brass bed. In her dreams, she'd spent the entire night there with him. She did *not* need more time with him today, especially not when she was so emotional over her son. She would just leave Hank a message on his voice mail once she got in her car.

She slipped the floral baby sling over her neck and settled her sleeping son inside. Today's blood work would bring them one step closer to having the surgery behind them. Two days from now, her son would have the procedure and life could return to normal.

Whatever *normal* was anymore.

She backed out the door, working her key down the locks. Hank's warning about the neighborhood, about providing for her child, tugged at her conscience. She turned around and pulled up short.

Hank sat on her top step. No *Top Gun* flight jacket today. He wore jeans and a button-down, loafers without socks. Old-school aviator glasses rested on top of his head without making a dent in his close-cropped brown hair. He had a casual air that worked for him without even trying.

How did he pull that off this early in the morning?

"Uh, Hank, what are—"

He held up a hand, and he gripped his iPhone in the other hand as he…played a game? The squawk, squeak and explosion noises coming from the handheld increased until a final blast and victory tune filled the morning. Hank didn't fist pump, but he smiled before tucking away his phone and reaching for his coffee beside him.

Shoving to his feet, he dusted off his jeans and slid his sunglasses down from his head and in place over his eyes. "Are you ready?"

She was so jangled from the explicit images of her dreams that she felt them simmer through her even now. She couldn't seem to draw a breath, as if just having him here stole all the air around her. Fighting for some distance, she shot him a level gaze and hoped her emotions didn't show.

"How long have you been there, and how did you get past the front gate?" She eyed the wrought-iron entry at the top of the alley. Still locked up tight. She looked back at Hank. "Well?"

"I've been waiting for twenty-five minutes to go with you to the doctor's appointment. As for how I got in, suffice it to say I've made my point about security." He drained his coffee cup with a final long swallow.

"Fine, you're right." She sighed and yanked off the diaper bag. She thrust it against his chest. "Make yourself useful and carry this."

Grabbing the handrail, she started down the stairs.

"Yes, ma'am." He laughed softly, his footsteps sounding behind her.

His laughter taunted and turned her inside out all

at once. God, he made her mad at the way he assumed he could thrust himself into her life, and she was even madder at herself for the leap of excitement over finding him waiting for her. "My car's parked in a lot a block away."

"I have my car right out front. I'll drive." He took her keys from her hand and opened the wrought-iron gate.

"You don't have an infant seat."

"Wrong. I do." He palmed her waist, guiding her past the shopkeeper sweeping beads and other Mardi Gras tokens littering the sidewalk.

"It's not even eight in the morning. Did the Renshaw-Landis influence make a baby seat appear in the night?"

He peered over the top of his aviator shades, blue eyes piercing and too darn appealing. "I went to Walmart Supercenter. Open twenty-four hours."

"Renshaws shop at Walmart?" She closed the gate behind her, stepping into her sleepy city and aware from the draw of just a look from Hank.

"For a car seat at midnight. Yeah." He pitched his coffee cup into a street trash can, then fished keys from his pocket and thumbed the automatic lock. Lights flashed on a dark blue Escalade. Not tricked out. Just understated wealth.

"Nice," she conceded. "Definitely more comfortable than my five-year-old little hatchback."

Forcing him to fold himself into her tiny econo car would be silly and pointless. In fact, fighting him every step of the way could be more telling than just going with the flow, pretending they were still simply friends.

He opened the back door and tossed in the diaper bag. "And does the infant seat meet with your approval?"

"Let me see...." She checked the belt, making sure he'd installed it properly.

"The air force trusts me with a B-52. I think you can trust me to follow instructions."

"It's my child's safety. I have to be sure." And she found nothing wrong.

Wow. It had taken her three hours to figure one of these out. She eased Max from the sling, her son so small in her hands, so perfect. Love and protectiveness welled up inside her—along with gratitude that Hank had gone to such trouble to make sure her baby had everything he needed.

Hank had to be exhausted, just back from overseas, then immediately on the road to see her. No wonder he needed the coffee. Her mouth watered at the thought of having a taste of something she'd been denied since getting pregnant with Max....

Uh, coffee. She missed coffee and chocolate and spicy foods, things she gave up while breastfeeding.

"Gabrielle?" Hank stood in the open door, her beautiful historic city behind him.

Her adventure. She'd started out here with such plans for taking the world by storm, launching a powerful career in international banking. Now she just wanted to help her child get healthy.

"Right, let's go before we're late."

She clicked Max in securely and thought about staying in back with him. But he was already asleep again and Hank was holding the passenger door open for her. Without another thought, she shuffled into the front, and Hank pulled out into the early morning traffic.

His GPS spoke softly. Of course he'd already plugged in the address for the hospital where Max would have his pre-admission blood work. Outside the car, people walked to work in business clothes. A mom pushed her kid in a stroller, passing by a homeless guy sleeping in a doorway. New Orleans was such a mix of history and wealth, poverty and decay. The city had looked different to her before her son was born. Her plans had looked different.

Hank's phone chimed from where he'd placed it on the dash. He glanced at the LED screen and let it go to voice mail. It was the same phone she'd seen him playing with earlier.

"I wouldn't have pegged you as the video game type."

He glanced over with barely a half smile, so serious for a guy who'd been blasting digital bugs on her steps. "I went to a military high school. One of my roommates was a computer geek."

"He got you hooked on games?"

"You could say so. His computer access was limited in school—conditions of not going to jail for breaking into the Department of Defense mainframe."

Her eyes zipped to his phone. "How did I never know you attended a military high school? Or that you're into video games?"

"You and I spent most of our time together keeping things light."

They had always avoided more serious subjects, like where they'd gone to school and their family histories. Until that day she'd poured her heart out over her fight with Kevin. How he'd wanted her to move in and she'd wanted the space to finish pursuing her dreams. Kevin had been living his. She just wanted the same chance.

She'd stopped short of telling Hank everything the fight had been about, unable to bring herself to share intimate details about a forgotten condom. How she'd been frustrated about Kevin's partying. The very playful attitude she'd originally been drawn to was beginning to pall. She was tired of always having to be the responsible one.

But God, she couldn't break up with Kevin right before a deployment, especially not when she wasn't even sure what she wanted. Talking to Hank, the harder she'd cried, the more she'd gasped, the more each breath hauled in the scent of him. Before she could think, she'd been kissing him, stunned as hell over the desire combusting inside her. She'd been attracted to him—sure—but she'd thought she had that under control. She was focused. She and Kevin were a good match. They balanced each other out, his humor lightening her driven nature. She didn't need more intensity in her life.

Except when Hank had focused all that intensity on her, she'd been damn near helpless to resist.

Her hands fisted until her gnawed-down nails bit into her palms. Their past time together was better left alone, especially today with everything he'd said last night still so fresh and raw. "Back to the DoD hacker high school roommate?"

"Once he turned twenty-one and got free of his cyber watchdog, he set up a small company that developed cutting-edge software. Computer games. Mostly save-the-world type of stuff."

"What game were you playing this morning?" she asked, intrigued by this side of Hank she hadn't guessed at before. Had he never seemed lighthearted around Kevin because Hank had been relegated to the role of mature grown-up? Had she lost some of *her* lightheartedness around her fiancé for the same reason, playing less rather than more around him? "Maybe I've heard of it."

"It isn't out yet."

"How nice of your friend to let you test run his material."

"I own part of the company."

That caught her up short.

"Really? Yet another thing I didn't know about you."
Did his influence stretch to every niche of the strato-
sphere—political, financial, military and now even the
geek-squad world, as well?

"I'm a silent partner, and I prefer to keep it that way.
I've got enough notoriety hanging around my neck thanks
to my family."

"Why this investment, though?" She wished she could
see his eyes, read what he was thinking as her impression
of him altered. "You're not a games kind of guy."

"But I'm a practical guy." He stopped smoothly at a
red light. "The venture made good business sense."

The MBA part of her applauded him, although she suspected something else was at work here. "You're all about
the military, not business. You don't care about money.
You never have." Her more frugal upbringing applauded
that, as well. "You risked the money to help a friend, and
it just turned out well for you."

"When did you swap from a business major to psy-
chology?" He slid his sunglasses down his nose, his eyes
laser sharp as he looked over the top of the lenses at her.

What a time to remember a blue flame burned hottest.

"Hey, you inserted yourself into my life. Turnabout is
fair play."

And damned if he wasn't doing it with complete ease.

This wasn't as easy as it seemed.

Midday sun piercing his aviator shades, Hank slid into
a parking spot two blocks away from Gabrielle's apartment. He'd spent all morning helping through the pre-
hospitalization blood work for her baby to have surgery
tomorrow. There hadn't been a chance to speak over
lunch, not between juggling the kid back and forth. So
the day was slipping away and he still hadn't made any

headway in finding an opening to persuade her to stay with him during the kid's recovery. Every time he got close, something distracted him.

Like the way Max had cried when the lab technician stuck his tiny toe.

Hank had wanted to tuck the kid under his arm like a football and book it out of the hospital. Which was damn silly. They were just doing their jobs around here. This was all necessary to make the boy better.

Now, they were already back at her place again. It was just past lunchtime, but felt as if it were even later. The kid was getting cranky, so Hank just unsnapped the car seat fast and hefted it out for expediency's sake. Gabrielle followed efficiently, the dark circles of worry under her eyes even darker. Damn it, she needed more help than just someone carrying the kid and supplying a meal.

Accordion zydeco music swelled from a street café, although, strangely, the antiques shop below her apartment sported a closed sign. He was going to have to just ask her to stay with him. And she would say no. Then he would have to get pushy, which would piss her off. Hell, it would piss him off. But he wasn't wrong.

Being right didn't comfort him much.

He pushed open the iron gate to let her through, prepping his words and his will for the fight ahead once she had her son fed and asleep again.

Gabrielle gasped and pulled up short. Instinctively, he looked around for a threat—a mugger? Another drunk like last night? How could he have forgotten they were in downtown New Orleans—an undeniably cool place to party but not the safest city on the planet?

Grabbing her around the waist with one arm, he tucked her against him. "Gabrielle?"

Ah, hell. Her bottom nestled right against him, close,

intimate and too arousing. He took a breath and backed away. They had a cranky kid to take care of.

"Look," she said, pointing up toward her apartment.

He barely had time to process the sight of water pouring out from under her door before the front entrance to the shop burst open. A woman—probably in her fifties—rushed toward them wearing a 1920s flapper get-up. Which would seem strange somewhere else. But New Orleans was an "anything goes" kind of place. A name tag pinned to her chest declared her *Leonie,* and the costume actually made sense for an antiques store employee.

Gabrielle brushed past him and clasped the woman's hands. "Leonie, what's going on?"

"A water pipe burst." She peered around Gabrielle with undisguised curiosity chasing away her harried look for a moment. "But a more important question, who's this?"

"Leonie, this is Hank, a friend of mine." Gabrielle chewed her lip before continuing. "Hank, this is Leonie Lanier. She works part-time in the shop and helps me with Max."

Interesting that she'd left off the Renshaw last name and hadn't referred to him as Kevin's friend. "Nice to meet you, ma'am."

"You, too, Hank." She finally peeled her gaze away and back onto Gabrielle. "The broken water pipe flooded all three floors. It's horrible downstairs. Yours is mostly damage along the floors. Still, even if your place isn't a mess, they had to turn off the water."

Gabrielle pointed up at the flowing stream trickling under her door. "And what's that if the water's off?"

"Everything that happened before we turned off the main valve." She pressed a hand to her forehead, right over the beaded band. "We're not sure what caused it, but I'm sorry, sweetie. All the renters in the building have to find somewhere else to stay. The second I heard that, my heart just sank for you and this precious little guy. As if you don't have enough to fret about now."

For the first time in ten godforsaken months, life was cutting him a break. He wouldn't have to fight or argue with Gabrielle. Persuading her to come to the house he'd rented would be a cakewalk now.

He clasped her shoulder, securing his grip on the car seat still in his other hand. "Gabrielle doesn't have to worry about a thing. She can stay with me."

"I'll check in to a hotel," she said tightly, stubborn to the end.

"Do you really want your son exposed to the germs of a generic hotel room?" He asked, swinging the car seat slowly to lull the restless baby.

"Since when did you become a germaphobe?" She perched her hands on her hips, cinching in her simple black cotton sheathe. "I distinctly recall you bragging about eating bugs in survival training."

"I'm not an infant facing surgery."

"Are you trying to make me cry?"

"I'm trying to take care of you, damn it!"

Leonie cleared her throat.

Damn. He'd forgotten she was there, forgotten they were standing in the middle of a busy street.

"Gabrielle, sweetie—" Leonie hooked an arm with her "—the hotels, motels, everything's full because of Mardi Gras."

Deflating, Gabrielle leaned back against the wrought-iron gate. "Of course they are. I should have thought of that myself. What are you going to do?"

"Don't worry about me. Just focus on Max," the older woman said, a helluva lot more subtle in exerting pressure than he'd been.

Resignation mingled with frustration on Gabrielle's weary but so damn gorgeous face. "But Hank, aren't you staying in one of those germy hotels?"

"Leonie can have my room." He stifled a wince since he'd actually already checked out of the place. But he could find somewhere in this overbooked town. There were always rooms set aside for someone with the right amount of money. He pulled out his phone. "Trust me. I can handle this. By the time you feed the kid and pack your suitcase, I'll have us in a house and your friend Leonie will be taken care of, as well."

Okay, so technically, he already had the house, but he didn't want to push his luck by letting her know he'd been working toward this victory since last night.

She eyed him suspiciously, hitching the diaper bag up higher on her shoulder. "Did you have someone sabotage the plumbing?"

"I would have if I'd needed to." Might as well give her the truth on that. "But fate has been kind to me today."

Still, her eyebrows stayed pinched together. She wasn't buying the ease of his plan for a second.

"Fine. You've got me." He whipped off his aviators and pinched the bridge of his nose. "Yes, I have a place to stay here. I arranged it last night, and yes, I was hoping even then that you would stay there for the duration of Max's recovery. The plumbing issue just makes the decision a no-brainer for you."

Gabrielle shoved away from the gate, fished out her keys and mumbled, "It's not my brain I'm worried about."

Five

Back in Hank's Escalade an hour later, Gabrielle wished everything in her life was as easy to decide as where to spend tonight. With her son's surgery scheduled for tomorrow, staying with Hank for the evening truly was a no-brainer.

After speaking to Leonie, she had gone upstairs to pack her things and nurse her son while Hank carried her bags and baby gear to the car. Thank goodness the damage to her place had been minimal. Clean up would be easy and her most treasured items were safe—her scrapbooks and photos.

Hank had made a couple of trips up and down the stairs lugging her stuff. Packing for tonight at Hank's place, plus the two-day hospital stay hadn't been easy. Where would she go afterward? What would she do? She would face that when the time came. For now, she could only think of getting through tomorrow's operation. Just thinking of her son going into the operating room had her stomach in turmoil, fears and tears bubbling to the surface.

That had to be the reason her feelings were so out of control around Hank. Once she had the procedure finished and her son healthy, her mind would clear. She would be rational again.

Hank drove through the Garden District and she settled deeper into her seat, letting the beauty soothe her ragged nerves. She hadn't bothered to ask Hank where they were going. Undoubtedly, they would have to drive for a while to reach anything available. She refused to think of her soaked apartment and the damage. She would sort that out with insurance later.

Passing historic home after home, they drove farther away from her apartment, slower and slower as if Hank sensed the peace she drew from soaking in their surroundings. Since Max was born, there hadn't been time to indulge in sightseeing tours. Even when she took her son for walks in his stroller, she was usually dead on her feet.

Like now, and it wasn't even suppertime yet.

Maybe she should ask Hank to swing into a drive-through on the way since she'd forgotten to eat breakfast. She looked over at him just as he turned the steering wheel, except he was pulling into a driveway not onto a road.

"Hank?" She sat up straighter.

A narrow, freshly paved driveway stretched beside a pink stucco house with metal balconies—Italianate style—all restored to former magnificence. The yard, while not huge, was a large plot in an area where land was at a premium. The lawn and garden did justice to its

Garden District address. She could only imagine what the place would be like in the summer.

When she'd dreamed of coming to New Orleans for graduate school, this was just the sort of place she'd envisioned visiting, maybe having lunch or treating herself to a night at a bed-and-breakfast. As a military brat with an American dad and German mom, she'd grown up all around the world, nowhere ever feeling like home.

New Orleans oozed with history, *roots*.

"Is this a bed-and-breakfast?" She rested a hand on Hank's arm, then pulled back quickly. "What a great idea, more comfortable, like a home. I don't know why I didn't think of that."

"It's not a bed-and-breakfast." He steered around back to an empty parking area with a three-car garage. "It's a vacation rental home."

"I don't remember seeing a Realtor's sign." She looked over her shoulder but the street had disappeared from sight as he stopped at the back door.

"The owners aren't the type to advertise." He shut off the SUV. "They work through a Realtor who sets up rentals for people who need space and privacy. Politicians. Actors."

"This is, uh—" She settled on "—thoughtful and a little overwhelming."

"Don't sweat this." He hooked an elbow on the steering wheel. "Really. This is nothing for me. It was easy, and I won't even notice the expense. So don't give me credit I don't deserve."

She looked at his casual wear and his old-school aviators. She'd allowed herself to be distracted from who he was. "I forget about your family sometimes."

"Thank you." Smiling, he swept off his shades. "I'll take that as a compliment."

"It is. But this—" she gestured to the yard, the no-kidding *mansion*— "is really too much."

"It's already done, Gabrielle. I have a week and a half left on my leave time, and I've already arranged to spend it in this house." He spread his arms, sunglasses dangling from his fingers. "So either you walk inside with me, or I'm stuck staying in there all alone for a week and a half, which sounds like an awful waste."

Shaking her head, she reached for the door. "Why do you keep making it sound like I'm doing you a favor when it's obviously the other way around?"

He leaned back and put his shades on again, pulling away in more ways than just physically. "Call it survivor's guilt. It's a real bitch."

What a sad situation they were both in here, trying to do right by Max and Kevin even when all these reminders of the past had to be flaying him raw inside, too. She blinked away tears and squeezed his hand.

"That it is," she whispered. "That it is."

An hour later, Gabrielle set Max's car seat on the floor and sagged back against the door to her temporary bedroom. Although the word *bedroom* seemed sorely inadequate to describe the luxurious quarters. Not a modern suite, per se, as the integrity of the old home had been maintained.

Grateful for some space to regroup before she faced Hank again, she carried Max's car seat deeper into the room and placed it at the foot of the sleigh bed. The large queen-size frame filled the space between two floor-to-ceiling windows. Slate-blue linens with splashes of yellow in the bolsters called to her to sneak a nap.

A fat yellow love seat was tucked in a nook. Persian rugs stretched over refinished hardwood floors that still bore the marks of past use. The beauty of the place was in how the imperfections were maintained so the home looked restored rather than gutted.

From what she'd seen, the rest of the house sported more of a skeleton set-up of basic furniture, the dining room with an antique table and sideboard with a gilded mirror on the wall. The living room was accented with a sofa and a couple of wingback chairs, along with sconces on the carved mantel. Mammoth windows, with airy curtains that pooled on the floor, added a whisper of color here and there to the otherwise whitewashed walls.

But beyond that, it was clear Hank had ordered additional items just for this visit.

A connecting door was open to the nursery, completely decked out in toile and stripes—black, white and gray—the contrasting colors perfect for a baby, yet in keeping with the historic home.

Beyond just the decor, the practical angles had been addressed, as well—diapers, sleepers, baby blankets and a monitor.

A mahogany end table—by the love seat—was actually a mini-fridge with a crystal bowl of fruit on top. She opened the small refrigerator to find—of course—bottled water, juice and milk.

When they'd hung out before, with Kevin, she'd known Hank came from a wealthy family, but he never flaunted his money. And he'd certainly never mentioned his savvy investment in a computer games venture. So this lavish display caught her off guard.

It also touched her.

Hank had given her time to unpack and then they planned to meet for supper. He'd ordered out and said they could dine on the side lanai. She had to admit, she welcomed the chance to soak up every wonderful detail of this dream home in her dream city.

With all Hank's help, she actually had time to take a more leisurely bath than the rushed shower she'd snagged in the morning.

She peeked into the bathroom and nearly groaned in ecstasy. Her gaze zipped right past the polished pewter-and-crystal fixtures to the deep claw-footed tub that lent an air of history, while spa jets inside the tub shouted pure modern decadence. She whipped her shirt over her head and ditched the rest of her clothes faster than she could think *Jacuzzi*—

Her cell phone chimed from her bedroom.

"Damn it," she whispered, then all but kicked herself. Before long, Max would be parroting everything she said.

She grabbed a thick, fluffy towel and wrapped it around herself on the run back into her bedroom. She couldn't afford to ignore ringing. What if it was a message from the hospital or Max's doctor?

Struggling to hold the towel in place, she fished through the diaper bag—like finding something in a deep black hole. Finally, her fingers closed around her cell and she yanked it free.

Her mother's number flashed on the caller ID. Relief warred with frustration. Already, she could imagine all the ways her mom would push her to come home.

She mentally switched to German and answered, "Hello, Mama."

"Why aren't you answering your phone at your apartment?" her mother asked, rapid fire and frantic. "I was worried sick some criminal had come in off the street and killed you both."

"I can assure you we're alive and not being held hostage by someone looking to hock my seventeen-inch television and costume jewelry."

Although she did have her diamond engagement ring, tucked away in a box and waiting for Max to give to his future wife one day.

"Well, if you're not being held at knifepoint and you're not dead in a ditch, then you were out all day. Too long for you to be out with a baby. Did your old car break down? You know your father could help you with things like that if you lived here."

She looked around the room and thought of how convoluted it would be to tell her mother everything going on with Hank right now. Especially when *she* wasn't even sure what was going on with Hank.

"Sorry, Mom, I just couldn't get to the other phone before you hung up."

"Tttt, ttt," her mother reprimanded. "You never were good at lying."

"Sheesh, I'm not ten anymore." She sank to the edge of the bed. "A water pipe broke in my apartment. My place is unlivable at the moment, so I had to find somewhere else to stay."

"My God, now of all times? Where are you?" Her mom still felt the need to keep tabs on all five of her kids, as if that would give her more control over a world where her husband got called away to secret locales at the drop of a hat.

In a way, Gabrielle got it. She wanted control over her own life now, too.

"I'm staying at a bed-and-breakfast."

Hopefully this time her lie played better to her mom's radar ears.

"A bed-and-breakfast? That sounds nice, almost as good as being home." Her mother's voice edged down a notch. "I just wanted to check on you. You promise you will call after Max's surgery."

"Of course I will." As a mother herself, she could well imagine how freaked out her mom must be right now. If only she could just be less...pushy about her own fears. It shouldn't take an entire ocean to create boundaries wide enough. "I know you're worried, too."

"I would be there, if you let me."

"Thank you, and I appreciate that. Honestly. But you already came out when Max was born." And when Kevin had died. Although she didn't want to talk about death, especially not tonight. "Thank you, Mama, but really, I'm managing okay."

Thanks to Hank.

Guilt pinched again over not being completely truthful with her mother. Her mom was an amazing woman, other than that "dead in a ditch" syndrome. She was a military wife, mom of five, two of which were still in junior high. She worked as a math teacher, swapping schools every time they moved. Her mother was so darn near close to perfect it was overwhelming sometimes.

Like now.

Gabrielle needed the space to be less than strong, less than perfect. She needed to just be upset for her child without worrying about making her mother even more smothering.

"Thank you for calling, Mama. But I should get some supper." And put on some clothes.

"Hold on just a few more minutes. Your father wants to say hello, too."

Gabrielle mentally switched to English to speak with her dad. She pictured her wiry, energetic mom zipping up all three flights of stairs in their fourplex searching. Gabrielle could hear her mom's repeated calls of "Gary!"

As a kid, she'd had nightmares about her burly, invincible dad dying in a war. Some of her mom's "dead in a ditch" syndrome had rubbed off. She'd grown up torn between a deep respect for those who wore a uniform and a desperate wish for her father to be someone different from who he was.

Even her perfect mother cried when she thought no one was looking.

Gabrielle gripped the phone tighter, questioning for the first time if she'd stayed in New Orleans for practical reasons—or because she hadn't wanted her family to see her grief.

"Gabby girl." Her dad's rumbly voice traveled through the connection, strong and familiar.

"Hello," she said to her father just as a tap sounded on the door. "Wait!"

She called out fast, but too late. The door was already opening after the hello.

"Ohmigod." She shot to her feet, towel gripped tight in her fist.

Hank stood in the open doorway, eyes wide. His feet were planted as if he was rooted to the floor in shock. He opened his mouth to speak, closed it and tried again. She held up a hand to silence him and damn near dropped her towel. She let the phone fall instead and grabbed fast to keep the towel in place.

Carefully, she knelt to pick up her cell without taking her gaze off Hank for a second. "Dad, love you tons, but I gotta go. Max needs me. I promise to call you and Mom tomorrow as soon as Max is out of surgery. Bye now."

She thumbed End Call, pitched the cell onto the bed and pressed both hands against the towel. Her body flamed to life at the stroke of Hank's eyes and yes, even more than that. Heat stirred because *she* saw *him*. More than just the breadth of his shoulders filling the doorway or his slim hips in khakis, she took in his face and, holy Gerard Butler, he was handsome in that rugged way made all the hotter by the keen intelligence in his blue eyes.

"Hank?" She cleared her throat and her thoughts. "Did you need something?"

Hank's slow, lazy blink spoke of hot sweaty sex. "Is there anything you need that hasn't been provided here?"

"Thank you, but we're fine. Everything's beyond perfect. I'll be down as soon as I get dressed." Although no way could she bathe now, not knowing that he would be thinking of her in the tub and she would be in that water thinking of how his eyes stroked her with unmistakable appreciation.

After months of pregnancy and postpartum body adjustment, she couldn't deny that his unhidden desire for her felt good. Who wouldn't be flattered, right? She was simply flattered.

Yet, the second he closed that door after him, her knees folded.

Hank sat on the lanai with a glass of sweet tea and listened to the distant sounds of a city that stayed awake late. Very late.

Draining his glass, he rocked the chair back and forth on two legs. He would have preferred a beer after the mind-blowing image of Gabrielle in nothing but a towel. Or maybe a few beers until he could pass out asleep rather than awake with the vision of her strolling through his mind every other second.

But he had to stay clearheaded and available in case she needed his help.

A dim light still shone from her room even well past— he checked his watch—one in the morning. She had to be dead on her feet after getting up with a kid all night, then the early start today. Not to mention the stress.

He'd already put into place a couple more plans for easing her life during Max's recovery. And damn it, there would be a recovery because Hank refused to accept any other outcome for tomorrow's surgery.

His chair legs slammed down on the porch.

He needed to check on her. Now. Find out why she couldn't sleep and see if there was something he could do. She'd been far too quiet at supper, eating in silence then excusing herself to go to bed. Except she still wasn't sleeping. Unless she left the lights on, in which case he would slip back out and grab some sleep himself.

These days he only managed about four hours of shut-eye anyway. That had started right about the time Kevin died. Hank was just wired. It would settle out as soon as he gained some closure by helping Kevin's kid.

A mocking voice in the back of his head reminded him he was here to see Gabrielle as much as the boy.

Hank strode quietly through the house. A good house. His stepbrother had done his standard stellar job on the place. A bit more furniture and it would be a worthy addition to the historic home tour circuit. He couldn't help but notice Gabrielle's appreciation. Felt good to get something right for her.

He took the stairs two at a time and stopped at the first door. Tapping once, twice, he waited…but no answer. He wasn't going to make the mistake of barging in on her again.

He started to turn away when the door opened. Gabrielle stood wide awake—and blessedly covered by a thick terrycloth robe. Max slept in her arms, his head on her shoulder.

Hank braced a hand on the frame, leaning toward her

without touching her. "Everything okay? Your light's still on. I thought you might need…a glass of water or something not here."

"There's water in the mini-fridge. The place has more amenities than I could have asked for." She rested her cheek on her son's head. "I just can't sleep. I need to hold him."

"Want some company?" The words fell out before he could rethink the wisdom of hanging out here in the late night with her.

Indecision flickered through her green eyes for a flash that had him thinking of emeralds. Nodding, she stepped back. "If we both can't sleep, might as well keep each other company."

Adjusting the baby on her shoulder, she curled up in a corner of the love seat. He dropped down beside her and waited. And waited. They used to talk for hours. Granted, they'd shot the breeze about lighthearted things or whatever was in the news. The one time they'd gone deep with the discussion he'd made the lame mistake of kissing her when he should have been comforting her.

He definitely needed to tread warily here.

Hank reached in the mini-fridge and pulled out a bottle of water, twisted off the top and set the drink beside her. "He's going to be okay."

"I know the odds are in his favor, but there's no way to be one-hundred-percent sure."

Grabbing a bottle of water for himself, as well, he nudged the door closed and leaned back, but the sofa brought them close, his leg pressed to her knees. He cleared his throat. "I looked into your doctors, and you're right, they're top notch."

She sat up straighter. "You investigated my son's doctors?"

"Shhh, you're gonna wake the kid." He waited until Max settled back to steady, sleepy breaths. "And yes, I wanted to check into them."

"You wanted to see if your money could bring something better." Her mouth pressed tight.

"Is that so wrong?" Although even if she thought it was, he would do it all over again. "Would you have turned me down on principle even if it meant settling for less for your kid?"

"Don't you think I already investigated them? As for the cost, I would have begged, borrowed or stole anything to make sure he gets the best possible care. I appreciate all you've done, but this is *my* child."

There was no mistaking the steel in her voice.

"I realize he's not my son, but he's my last link to Kevin. That means something."

You mean something.

The words hung out there, unspoken, but implied.

Understood.

She reached to touch his arm lightly, lingering. "It's hard for me to let people do things for me. My mom is a wonder woman in every sense of the word." She rolled her eyes. "I struggle to get both Max and myself showered by noon."

"You looked beautiful—and clean—this morning." He dipped to sniff her neck. "You smell good, like flowers, the purple kind. I think you're good on the hygiene."

She laughed. "Okay, technically clean since showers happen. Fast, of course…. The flowers are lavender. It's supposed to be relaxing."

He laughed along with her even though she was killing him with images of her soaked under the spray, and he found the sweet scent of her anything but calming.

Her fingers twitched on his arm. It was such a soft

touch, nothing overtly sexy with the kid around and her fears so thick he just wanted to haul her close until the next twelve hours could pass.

Her hand slid away. "You come from a family of amazing women, too. Your sisters juggle kids and military careers. Your stepmom was the Secretary of State, for goodness' sake. I've never even actually met them, and I'm already in awe. And then you've got all those stepsiblings...."

"Do you see now why I hide out here in Louisiana?"

"Hiding out? I can understand that." She winked at him with a splash of her old spunk shining through the exhaustion. "What about your mother? I've never heard you mention her."

"I don't remember a lot about my mom. She died when I was still in elementary school."

"And?" she prodded gently.

He didn't dwell on his childhood. Thinking about it wouldn't change a thing. But if that's what Gabrielle wanted to talk about, then fine. He would talk while walking on crushed glass if that would help her get through the night.

"One Christmas, my oldest sister made a photo album for me and for our other sister with all the family pictures taken before Mom died, some pictures from when she was a kid, too. There are days I'm not sure what memories are real and what's been created by those images."

"Does it matter if you remembered them or if she helped remind you of things you did together? I think it was a beautiful thing your sister did, gathering that together, helping you hold on to those moments you shared with your mom."

"Yeah, I guess. Better to have those memories than none at all. For some reason, both my sisters seem to remember more." And little Max would have no memories of the father he'd never even met. Hank rethought the concept of being "all in." This kid would need him for more than the next two weeks. Hank was a crucial link to memories of Kevin, especially if Kevin's parents were checking out. And who else would explain about Kevin's military service, how much he loved to fly?

"Hank." Her voice pulled him back to the moment. "What do you remember, beyond those photos?"

And just that fast, Gabrielle sent him into a fugue world between now and then, fusing the two. "I remember the sound of her voice when she read the *Gingerbread Man* at Christmas. To this day, the smell of gingerbread makes me think of her."

"That's a great memory of her to carry." She cupped his face, her eyes filled with compassion for him, even in the middle of her own crisis.

God, she was killing him here. He had to touch her back.

He grazed his knuckles along her cheek. "I guess what I'm trying to say is Max isn't going to care if you've got on makeup by lunch. When he thinks of his mom, he's going to think of the love in your voice."

Before he knew that he'd moved or she'd moved, she was leaning into his arms. Her back rested against his chest, his arms going around her and the baby.

She was right. He couldn't promise her everything would work out tomorrow. But he could damn well be there to hold her through the night.

Six

As the morning ticked away on the hospital clock, Gabrielle took comfort from Hank's arm around her shoulders. He'd been at her side on the waiting room sofa since the surgery started a half hour ago.

He'd been with her through the night each time she woke to feed Max, as well. His thoughtfulness—and the intimacy—wrapped around her as firmly as his arm. Why was it she could relax into Hank's comforting presence but not in her own family's?

She'd been so determined to face this on her own, and yet here Hank stayed, helping. And she couldn't deny his presence made things easier. She couldn't fathom what it would be like to sit here alone in this waiting room interspersed with others clinging to each other for support.

Although, if the surgery had occurred a few days earlier, she *would* have been here by herself to face the sterile air of fear and dying flowers. Somehow she'd lost sight of the fact he'd only just returned from a war zone.

Her head on his shoulder, she looked up at his deeply tanned face. "You must have had bigger plans for your homecoming than babysitting a distraught mom."

A smile fanned creases in the corners of his eyes. "My plans mostly consisted of food and sleep, so I'm good."

"What kind of food?" she pressed, needing the sound of his voice to fill the awful silence. It had been so hard walking away from Max this morning, leaving her precious boy in someone else's care to face the ordeal.

"Anything not cooked in a mess hall or prepackaged as an M.R.E." He lifted his foam cup. "And real coffee."

She inhaled the fresh roast scent steaming upward. "I hear you on that. I'm looking forward to knocking back an espresso someday. How ironic that when a mom needs the extra jolt from caffeine most, it's not good for the baby."

"Hadn't thought of it that way." He set aside his cup. "Anything else you're looking forward to getting back to once Max is healthy?"

"I haven't really thought about much but him. Looking into the future has been scary."

"You're going to be making plans before you know it." He squeezed her shoulder, drawing her closer to the warm press of his body against her side. "Why not get a head start? Today's for positive thinking. What are you going to do for yourself?"

The answer popped to mind fast, but it wasn't fancy and so very much *not* a guy thing that she held back. "You're going to laugh if I tell you."

"Me? Laugh at you? Not a chance in hell." The steady hold of his blue eyes reassured her.

"My wishes aren't lavish like your family's."

He tugged a lock of her hair. "Haven't you figured out yet that I'm the black sheep of the group? I prefer to fly under society's radar, so to speak."

From what she knew of him, that entirely fit. He was a man of grounded values. She'd always liked his lack of pretentions in light of such an illustrious pedigree. "Okay, when I'm playing, I like to do things that are totally different from my analytical MBA studies, totally hands-on rather than techno, like the computer work."

"What would that be?"

"Scrapbooking."

His forehead pinched in confusion. "Scrapbooking... Like...photo albums?"

"You are such a guy." She patted his chest—a flipping brick wall. Gulp.

"Your point?"

She laughed softly, so very grateful for the way he distracted her from her worries, from things she had no control over right now. "I've always held on to keepsakes. Moving around so much, I wanted something tangible from people in each city. With my father gone so much, I also wanted to be sure I didn't lose a single memory we made together. I collected ticket stubs, pictures, pressed flowers—filling up shoeboxes. Eventually it needed organizing and labeling."

"My mom would really like that." He nodded, his hand sliding along her shoulder to massage her neck. "My stepmom, too, for that matter. She has rows of shelves with photo albums. Now that I think about it, I've seen her with some of the wives and grandkids messing with photos and stamps."

"Scrapbooking has become an art form, with special papers and stickers and stamping." She resisted the urge to moan in pleasure at the magic of his fingers along the knotted tendons in her neck. "Some people make their own greeting cards—real works of art."

"And you get a creative outlet to balance your more analytical work." He pointed to a nurse walking past with a stack of charts. "Like how she has that funky fabric cover over part of her stethoscope.

"Exactly." How cool that he got it, rather than just dismissing her hobby as keeping junk—like Kevin had once said.

"I would guess you've started a scrapbook for Max... and have one about Kevin."

"Yes to both." She needed to capture those happy memories for herself and to share them with her son. "When my apartment flooded I was so scared something had happened to them."

"Are they okay?"

She nodded. "Completely undamaged. I boxed them up when I packed clothes for Max and me."

"What will go in the book for today?"

"Max's hospital bracelet. The appointment slip you saw on the refrigerator." She envisioned the page taking shape. "I'll stamp it with a stethoscope symbol maybe, and perhaps tack down the info with Band-Aids on the corners."

"And your book about Kevin?"

"You keep mentioning that." She pushed down feelings of disloyalty. It wasn't as if she was cheating on Kevin by sitting here with Hank. "I would rather not talk about him today."

"Why not?"

She leaned forward, grabbed his wrist and inched away. "Because it makes me uncomfortable to discuss him when you have your arm around my shoulders."

"Oh, really?" He gestured to the older couple across

from them. "He has his arm around her. Doesn't look like a big deal to me. Just comfort. Unless you're telling me you feel something more than that when we touch."

The air between them crackled with how easily comfort could lead to something far more physical. It was one thing to feel it without acknowledging it. But labeling the attraction for what it was—desire—that scared her. And right now, she didn't have the emotional reserves to play games or snap back with some witty answer that would deflect the issue.

She leaned in closer, lowering her voice so no one else would hear. "Is that what *you* feel when you put your arm around me? The need to comfort?"

"Yes, and more." He tucked a knuckle under her chin. "What about you?"

God, she couldn't lie to him or to herself anymore. "Yes, and more."

His hand slid behind her neck again, and he kissed her. Just lightly, a skim of his mouth over hers in a totally appropriate way for their surroundings. Anyone else would see them as a couple, connected and caring for each other. He rested his forehead against hers and she squeezed her eyes shut, her heart hammering in her ears, blood stinging her veins. She gripped his hard muscled arms and just held on, grateful to have him here. Confused about everything except the fact that she could not tell him to leave. Hank had a way of sliding into her life like a clean-fit piece to a puzzle.

So she simply sat, holding on to him while she said prayers for her child and drew in the steadying scent of this vital man who'd charged into her life again.

The sound of approaching footsteps drew her up sharply.

"Ms. Ballard?" the surgeon in scrubs called, walking toward her.

Her stomach clenched, and she instinctively reached for Hank's hand. He linked fingers with her without hesitation.

"Yes, Doctor Milward?"

"Your son came through the operation without any complications…."

The surgeon continued speaking, but the words blurred in the pool of relief flooding her. She sagged back and Hank's arm was right there to brace her, a solid wall of support, just like the man. But for how long?

Now that her child's surgery was successfully completed, so was Hank's role as stand-in dad.

For the past two days, he'd worked his tail off to be a stand-up guy for Gabrielle while Max recovered in the hospital. He'd brought her favorite local muffuletta sandwiches and changes of clothes. She'd slept in a chair by her son's bed—and he used the term *sleep* lightly. The circles under Gabrielle's eyes had deepened.

His plans to lighten her load needed to step up a notch before she collapsed.

At least now that Max had been discharged, she hadn't argued about coming back to the Garden District house with him. He stood in the doorway to the nursery, watching her swap out Max's diaper and put on a fresh onesie— Yeah, he knew the word *onesie* now, something he hadn't picked up from his nieces and nephews.

He took in the way her green cotton dress swirled around her legs as she moved, the glide of her silky blond hair as she leaned over the changing table to coo nonsensical phrases to her son. The joy on her face almost managed to chase away those lines of exhaustion. Regardless, right now, the glow of love and happiness radiating off her damn near blinded him. She was beyond beautiful. She was... He didn't even know the words or the label.

Not surprising. She'd turned his world upside down all over again.

The brief kiss they'd shared at the hospital had shifted something between them—actually, he would say the change started the night before Max's surgery when he'd held her until daylight. There was an acceptance of each other's presence, an ease to the way they spoke. More than one person at the hospital had mistaken them for a couple. And he knew before much longer he was going to have to think about that.

For now, though, he was focused on making sure *she* didn't end up in the hospital. Thinking of anything beyond that would place him firmly in jackass territory.

He rapped his knuckles lightly on the open nursery door. "Hello, gorgeous."

She looked up and smiled self-consciously, lifting her son to her shoulder and patting his back. "You mean, 'Hello, haggard.' But I'm cool with that. It's all worth it now that Max is home."

Home? He didn't even consider correcting her. "I've got supper downstairs. There's a porta-crib set up so you can keep him close. Unless you would rather just call it a day. I can bring something up to you."

"You've already done more than enough for me. I'm going to get spoiled."

"My sisters say all new moms deserve pampering."

Her smile faded. "Hank, I'm truly grateful, but you don't have to do all of this for me because of Kevin."

"What if this isn't about Kevin?"

She didn't move, barely blinked, her eyes locked with

his. His words hung there between them, linking them as surely as if he'd taken her hand. Or more.

"Uhm—" she chewed her bottom lip for a second "—you mentioned something about supper."

While she'd neatly avoided the topic, he took it as a victory of sorts that she didn't argue.

"Right, I did." He shoved away from the door frame. "Follow me."

He led her down the lengthy staircase, through the library and opened the double French doors out to the lanai. Live music from a party next door drifted along the evening breeze. A Cajun band played as the neighbor apparently sought to stretch Mardi Gras out even longer.

"I set up Max's porta-crib here in the corner. If we leave the doors open, you can see him from the table." He extended his hands. "Pass him to me, and I'll put him down."

She froze. What a time to realize he'd never held the kid. Surely he must have? At some point in the hospital, in passing? But the more he searched his memory, the more he realized, nope, he hadn't. Was it because she hadn't offered or because he'd never asked?

Slowly, she eased Max from her shoulder and placed him in Hank's outstretched hands. Holy crap, the kid was tiny and so damn fragile. He'd always thought his siblings were nuts when they pointed out how their newest offspring had somebody's nose or smile. But right now, he could see his friend in Max's eyes.

Hank put the boy into his crib, careful to position him just like Gabrielle did, but needing some distance from those familiar eyes.

Gabrielle tipped her head to the side. "Everything okay?"

"Sure," he said past the lump in his throat. "Let's step outside to eat."

The table for two had been set with flowers and a candle in a hurricane globe. A cart held their supper and dessert.

She lifted the silver lids on the chafing dishes one at a time, sniffing and sighing at the savory gumbo, crab cakes, all warmed by a flame underneath.

Pulling a chair out for her, he waited for her to sit. "I had the chef go light on the spices. These are things you've ordered in the past, so I figured it was a safe bet. There's a backup in the refrigerator, though."

"Another muffuletta?" Her eyes twinkled at just the mention of the super large, round sandwich with salami, mozzarella and olives.

"In a heartbeat, if you wish."

She paused by the chair, her head tipped into the wind. "Actually, you know what I would really like?"

"Name it." He would find it, buy it, build it, whatever necessary.

"Could we dance?" She swayed to the slower beat of a Cajun fiddle solo. "The music is amazing. It seems a crime not to make the most of it."

To hell with supper. He opened his arms. She stepped into his embrace, her hand fitting into his. His palm molded to the small of her back and with each step around the lanai, she relaxed closer and closer. Under his touch, the tension eased from her body. She hummed along softly with the tune, the vibration of her voice sweet against his fingertips.

She took such pleasure from such a simple thing—a dance and someone else's music. He wished he could shower her with more than just nice meals and a shoulder to lean on. The way she worked so hard, building a world for her son out of thrift store finds and scraps of memories pasted into books—well, it damn near broke his heart. He considered himself a practical man, but right now, he was feeling anything but sensible. She deserved spa days to recharge, a home like this.

A man in her life to help shoulder the load.

Next door, couples danced, friends partied at the catered event. A corner of the other lawn was open to view. Sprawling oak trees were lit up with twinkling lights. Sure the party was raucous, but not a huge gala. Rather, family and friends had gathered—much like the sort of thing his dad had said they wanted to throw for him, the sort of shindig he usually avoided.

And now?

He definitely didn't want his family around questioning what was going on here with Gabrielle. He wouldn't even know how to answer other than to say that he wanted her and couldn't walk away. But it wasn't as if they were actually dating. There was so much mixed up here to be sorted out. She'd loved Kevin. And yeah, he couldn't stop the sting of guilt from being here in place of his friend.

Her fingers circled along the back of his neck. "Thank you for this, for the past few days, as well. You truly made this so much easier for me than I could have imagined."

"That's what I'm here for." Being a stand-in for Kevin, even when it sliced him raw, because right now, he wanted to know that Gabrielle saw *him,* not a replacement for the man she mourned.

"I probably should have accepted my parents' offer of help. I really do love my mom, but she takes over rather than helping, and since everything's a battle, I end up even more exhausted."

"I get what you mean." His feet moved in perfect sync

with hers, his thoughts, too. "My dad casts a helluva large shadow."

She leaned back to look into his eyes, the wind lifting her hair. "So why did you choose to go into the same branch of the service, even the same aircraft he flew?"

"It's what I want to do. Call it genetics, if you will, but it's what I'm good at." He couldn't imagine doing anything else with his life. "Seems ridiculous to pick something that's not my first choice simply to go a different path."

"I can see that."

He rested his chin on the top of her head, breathing in the scent of lavender and pure Gabrielle. "Although, I gotta confess, it would have made life easier."

"Kevin told me you work twice as hard as everyone else trying to prove you didn't get anything because of nepotism—when it's clear to everyone you're a freakin' rock star at your job."

"A rock star, huh?" He could almost hear his friend's voice through her and, God, he missed Kevin.

"He said some folks knew the science of aviation and navigation, but you knew the art."

"His opinion means a lot to me. Thanks for sharing that."

Was Hank ever going to get past the way their lives linked up? Be able to look at Gabrielle without thinking of Kevin? Sure his buddy had been a lighthearted guy, but there'd been no missing how much he'd loved Gabrielle. He'd taken his commitment to her seriously.

Not that any relationship was perfect.

One night, Kevin had gotten drunk and rambled about how much he loved Gabrielle but worried about being the kind of man who could make her happy. He didn't want to lose her, but she wanted roots and a home.

What a kick in the butt to remember that right now since Hank didn't have anything different to offer her on that front. "Kevin really loved you."

She stiffened in Hank's arms, each breath warm against his neck as she continued to silently follow his dance lead.

"I was with him when he bought the ring." A day that had damn near ripped his soul out. He clasped her left hand and brought it between them, her ring finger bare. "He called your mom to get your size and some direction on what you wanted."

Her heart beat faster against their clasped hands. "I wore it on my right hand for a while after he died. I had to take it off at the hospital when Max was born, and I haven't put it on since. I've stored the ring for Max to give his wife one day."

"I'm sure Kevin would like that." He actually hadn't agreed with the ring Kevin and her mom had chosen. He would have picked something simpler, more in keeping with her streamlined style. But she'd seemed happy and that's what mattered.

"You really were a great friend to him. You still are."

"Other than making out with his fiancée."

She stopped dancing and took his face in her hands. "I'm the one that kissed you. I'm the one who deserves the blame."

"You really think you started that?" He gripped her wrists but couldn't bring himself to lower her arms, her cool touch enticing him even with his conscience chewing him up inside.

"I know I did, because I was eaten up with guilt over being attracted to you." Her fingers unfurled, and she swayed toward him. "Not just that one day, but weeks prior to that."

"Weeks?" He brought her closer.

"It wasn't some massive event that changed things. Just one evening we were on a riverboat dinner cruise and you were standing by the rail." She leaned into him, her eyes glimmering with tears and confusion. "Something just shifted inside me, something scary. But Kevin was so close to deploying. How could I tell him then? He and I wouldn't have had time to sort through anything before he left. I wasn't even sure what I felt for you. Then that day I fought with Kevin, cried in your arms…"

"You only acted on something I'd been feeling from the first day I met you. Once you kissed me, believe me, I was one-hundred-percent all in."

Her eyes went wide with surprise—and an answering hunger. Unable to resist her now any more than he'd been able to then, he dipped his head. He kissed her. He had to. Since he'd come back to New Orleans, they'd been shadow boxing with this moment. But here, tonight, under the stars, he wanted her, and he could feel that she wanted him too from the way she wriggled to get closer. He couldn't sense even the least bit of hesitation in her response.

She looped her arms around his neck and pulled him closer, a perfect fit just like a year ago. Her lips parted, and he didn't need any further invitation to take the kiss deeper. He cupped her bottom and lifted her more securely against him until her toes left the ground.

Pivoting, he backed her against an ancient oak. Her fingers roved restlessly into his hair. The press of her body against his had him hard and throbbing in a flash. Her soft breasts against his chest made him ache to peel away their clothes.

Now that he had her against him again, the taste of her fresh on his tongue, he had to savor the moment for an extra stroke longer. With each pounding of his heart against his ribs, he knew he couldn't let her walk away again without taking this to completion. Ignoring the attraction hadn't worked, in fact, it had only increased the urgent need to explore every inch of her body with his eyes, his hands, his mouth.

A cry mingled with the music, bringing him up short. *Max.*

The infant's hungry wails grew louder.

Gabrielle froze in Hank's arms, then stepped away sharply. Her hands shook as she swept her hair back and rushed past him through the open French doors. He sagged back against a hundred-year-old oak and felt just about as ancient, the weight of what he'd almost done bearing down on his shoulders.

He couldn't—shouldn't—finish this, not tonight, not now when she was nearly dead on her feet with exhaustion. Her son had just gotten home from the hospital. She was feeling vulnerable. Only a selfish bastard would take what she offered and to hell with his conscience. She needed sleep—and they both needed to find a way to put Kevin's ghost to rest.

Because regardless of whether or not she wore that three-carat ring or not, Kevin's memory still stood firmly between them.

As the grandfather clock in the hall chimed midnight, Gabrielle stared at the blurry words on her computer screen, her foot lightly rocking her son's infant seat. The band still played next door, the neighbors' party going on into the night.

She wished she could blame her lack of focus on exhaustion, but she couldn't lie to herself, not tonight. While she should be catching up on work, her mind was too full of dancing with Hank.

Then he'd kissed her.

His mouth on hers, his hands on her body had felt every bit as earth-shattering as she'd remembered. So much so she'd almost forgotten about her son sleeping a few feet away. She'd grabbed her child and raced up the stairs, using Max's feeding as an excuse to gather her thoughts and composure.

Okay, hell, truth be told, she was hiding out in her room.

Once she'd fed and changed Max in the nursery, she'd come back to her room to find dinner had been brought to her. Dinner for one with a note from Hank.

See you in the morning.

He'd simply scrawled *H* for a signature, the stroke of the pen heavy and thick. Strong and bold like the man.

And smart. He'd been right to bring her food here and leave. They both needed space. So much was happening in such a short time.

Still, the meal had tasted bittersweet, each bite reminding her of how special the evening had started off. Dancing with him under the moonlight with live music lent a timeless air to the night. They could have been any couple, even centuries ago. Surely being any other couple would have made things less complicated.

Max's cry then reminded her of her responsibilities. She couldn't afford to forget them for a second. Rather than go to sleep after feeding her son, she'd parked her butt with her laptop computer to catch up on work she'd let slide while he was in the hospital.

The sooner she finished, the sooner she could sleep, and she would need a clear head to think through how she wanted to approach Hank in the morning.

Forcing her bleary eyes to focus, she clicked through the rest of her backlog of emails, then closed her computer. She glanced at her watch. One in the morning. With the time change, her mother should be waking up now.

Gabrielle shifted Max from his infant seat to his crib in the nursery so her conversation wouldn't wake him up. Still, she left the connecting door open so she could be sure to hear him.

Collapsing back into the pile of pillows and bolsters, she grabbed her cell phone off the bedside table and thumbed her parents' number. The billowy soft bed, the jazz music and the scent of Hank clinging to her dress stirred her already hyperaware senses.

The ringing on the other end stopped as her mother finally picked up.

Gabrielle clutched the phone tighter and rolled onto her side, staring out the window at the twinkling lights on the trees next door. "Hey, Mama, it's me."

"Is everything all right with Max? With you?" her mother asked in a panicked voice.

"Don't worry. Everything's fine." Empathy tugged at her heart. While she swore she wouldn't be as overpowering as her mom, she was starting to understand how easy it would be to let those parental fears take control. "I'm only calling to let you know Max is home from the hospital."

"Your apartment is fixed already?" The sounds of her cooking breakfast echoed in the background, clanking pots and water running, familiar sounds of home. "How perfect that could be taken care of while you were with Max."

"Uh, actually, I am staying with a friend."

"In New Orleans? Do I know this friend?"

"Him. Hank," she blurted out, even though telling her

mother was probably a totally stupid idea. And saying his name, admitting they were staying together, lent an importance to the relationship she wasn't sure if she could wrap her thoughts around just yet. "He's a friend of Kevin's. A friend of mine."

"Do I know this friend? This *man?*"

"Kevin's friend."

"Hank? As in Hank Renshaw, Jr.?" Most mothers would have been turning cartwheels over their daughter hanging out with one of America's most eligible bachelors, but there was no missing the censure in her mom's tone. "Gabrielle, are you sure now's the right time to get involved with anyone?"

Like she really had a choice? She couldn't ignore the truth now the way she had a year ago. Her attraction to Hank went way beyond friendship.

"Mama, I understand you're just worried, but I'm an adult, perfectly capable of handling my own life." She spoke quickly so her mother wouldn't be able to wedge a word in edgewise. "I love you, truly I do, but I need to hang up now and get some sleep. Give my love to Daddy and everyone else. Okay? Goodbye."

Gabrielle ended the call and tossed aside the phone, gnawing her lip. In less than two weeks Hank would report back to Barksdale Air Force Base. He would be hours away, and she would be back in her apartment. No. She needed to accept her life had changed. She couldn't live in this holding pattern. She would have to find a different, more kid-friendly place to live. And in order to do that on her limited budget, she would have to move outside the city limits. Time to shift out of the holding pattern she'd been living in.

Those changes included more than just her living situation. She needed to stop avoiding her attraction to Hank.

Starting first thing tomorrow, she would confront Hank.
No more pretending. No more avoiding.

She and Hank were meant to be lovers.

Seven

She ached to have him. Her flesh was on fire from months, years of wanting Hank.

And here in her dream world she could have him.

They could make love under a sprawling oak tree with twinkling lights that echoed the sparks of desire crackling through her. She could almost feel the silky inside of his leather jacket, spread on the ground beneath her. She could stroke and savor the hard planes of his chest as he loomed over her, thrusting into her, filling her, taking her so close to the edge of completion.

Her body burned for the fulfillment only he could offer. She moaned her need for him to take her the rest of the way there, not to leave her hungry, hurting, wanting....

Gabrielle bolted upright in bed, the scent of leather still lingering from her dream. Her dream that had been cut short before she'd reached satisfaction.

Blinking fast against the bright morning sun streaking through the window, she struggled to orient herself. She was alone in her bed, covers tangled around her legs. She kicked free of the sheets and her erotic images of Hank.

Or at least she tried to. The unfulfilled ache still lingered between her legs, echoing the near painful tingling in her breasts.

Her full and tender breasts.

Oh, God.

She pressed her hands to her chest and realized…it was morning, and she still wore her dress from yesterday. She'd fallen asleep just after hanging up with her mom. She hadn't fed Max since just before midnight.

Her son hadn't woken up.

Panicked, she shot from the bed and almost fell on her face tripping over the trailing comforter. Her heart lodged in her throat, fear threatening to strangle her. She raced across the room, past her damn computer that had kept her up so late. Had her son cried for her and she didn't hear him because of her exhaustion? Guilt tore at her. She ripped open the connecting door to the nursery, wondering how it could have drifted closed in the night without her hearing.

Her eyes homed in on the crib, the empty crib. A cry strangled in her throat. She looked around frantically until her gaze hitched on the corner rocking chair.

Her son was being held by…Leonie Lanier?

Max's babysitter—their neighbor from above the antiques shop—was here? And there were four empty bottles sitting beside the rocker, so she must have been feeding him the expressed milk Gabrielle had frozen and stored before the surgery. Gabrielle could hardly wrap her mind around what must have happened in the night.

She could only embrace the relief that her son was okay. She reached for Max. "Leonie, what are you doing here?"

Standing, her neighbor passed over the baby with a smile. "Helping you get a good night's sleep."

Gabrielle pressed five frantic kisses on her son's forehead. Her weak knees folded, and she sank into the rocking chair. Laying Max on her legs, she unsnapped his onesie and checked his three tiny incisions from the laparoscopic surgery. Her son squirmed in her arms, wide awake and cooing his "good morning" up at her as he pedaled his feet against her stomach.

Everything appeared to be fine, but he was her responsibility. Her son.

The trembling inside her wouldn't stop, months of stress and worry compounding. "That's very generous of you, but I wish someone would have told me. How long have you been here?"

Where was Hank? He had to know because only he could have let Leonie into the house. She hitched Max up to her shoulder.

"I arrived around ten last night. That cute Major Renshaw and I swapped off taking care of Max through the night. I've offered a million times, and you were always so stubborn about doing everything yourself." She crossed her legs, one tennis-shoe-clad foot swinging. She wore a track suit and looked surprisingly fresh for someone who'd cared for a baby all night. "Your friend and I decided to surprise you."

"Well, you certainly succeeded." Not in a good way. But she would save that frustration for later when she confronted Hank. That he would have gone behind her back... He'd even closed the door while she slept....

No wonder she'd been smelling his leather jacket. He'd been in her room.

Leonie sat on the daybed tucked against the window. "I really can't take credit for any generosity. Your friend knew the flooding put me out of my home, too—and I've lost my part-time job as long as the shop is closed. He offered me this position until I'm back to work, which is perfect since when I go back you'll be able to go back, too."

Position? "Hank's paying you?"

"Uh-huh. I already know Max's routine and I adore the little guy— Are you upset?"

"Surprised," she said tightly, patting Max on his back as he squirmed.

"Oh, my goodness, if I've overstepped, sweetie, let me know." Leonie's hazel eyes filled with concern. "It seemed like the perfect solution to all our problems and a great surprise for you."

"Of course it is. You haven't done anything wrong." Well, other than not speaking to her first, but chewing out Leonie wouldn't accomplish anything. Chewing out Hank, on the other hand, would make Gabrielle feel much better.… "Thank you for your help. You're one of the few people I feel comfortable with watching Max."

Max wriggled, his fingers getting tangled in her hair as he started to whimper with his "feed me" sounds.

"You do look better, more rested." She cupped Gabrielle's cheek. "That's a very good thing, even if you are still too tense. You're no help to Max if you wear yourself down until you're sick."

"You had the night shift, so how about I take him for a while? I need to nurse him." She worked free the front buttons on her dress and her son latched on, tiny fists flailing, then finally settling as he calmed. She stroked his

impossibly soft cheek with one knuckle, love and protectiveness flooding fiercely through her. "Actually, I need
to hold him. I'm sure it will take a while for the worry to
fade."

"You're a mama now." Leonie winked on her way out
the door. "You're never going to stop worrying."

Gabrielle sagged back in the chair, rocking faster, frustrated with herself as much as with Hank. Sometime last
night she'd allowed herself to get complacent, to take all
the help Hank had offered. She'd lowered her boundaries,
and while his intentions may have been good, he'd steam-
rolled right over her. Hiring a sitter for her son without
consulting her? Taking her son so she wouldn't hear him
wake up?

She'd been delusional thinking she could just jump
into an affair with Hank. Her life wasn't that simple. She
had concerns and responsibilities beyond what she could
have imagined a year ago.

Hank may not have changed, but she had.

Hank leaned back in the chair on the lanai, thumbs
flying over the game on his phone. The late-morning
sun beat down on his head. The clean-up crew next
door clanked trash cans. Hopefully, they weren't waking
Gabrielle. As hard as she'd been working the past months,
he couldn't imagine how much sleep would be enough.

If she didn't catch up on her rest soon, she would snap.
He'd heard the same advice in those end-of-deployment
briefings they all got at the end of each tour. Decompress.
Take time off. Play.

His thumbs flew faster over the video game, and he
wondered why the kink in his neck didn't ease even when
he hit the eighth level. If anything, the longer he spent
away from base, the itchier he got. Which likely had more

to do with the woman sleeping upstairs than any need to decompress.

The French doors swung open sharply. His chair slammed to the ground. He tossed his phone on the table just as Gabrielle charged through.

God, she was gorgeous and tousled.

And mad?

"A nanny?" She stopped short in front of him. "You hired a *nanny* for my son?"

Standing, he clasped her shoulders and resisted the urge to just kiss away her bad mood. "I thought you could use some sleep. I was being thoughtful, being a good... friend."

"Well, I'm being a mother, doing what a mother does. I'm taking care of my child." She swept a hand around her, gesturing to the historic home and gardens. "The house, the furniture, that's generous, thoughtful beyond belief, and I appreciate that you're trying to help. But you do *not* have the right to choose childcare for my son."

What the hell? He'd thought she would be turning back flips over a good night's sleep. "Is Max okay? Did something happen?"

"He's fine," she said tightly.

"Leonie Lanier is your regular babysitter. You've already chosen and approved her. I tossed some extra money at the situation." It's not like he would even miss the cash. "Consider it a baby gift since I wasn't here when he was born. So what's the problem?"

She ground her teeth, her fists clenched at her side. "You didn't ask me first."

"You're pissed at me?" He scrubbed a hand behind his neck.

"*Yes,* I'm angry."

His gift was definitely backfiring here. "Because I wanted to help you?"

"Because you made arrangements for my son—" she jabbed him in the chest with each phrase "—an infant, who just got out of the hospital, without discussing it with me first. You're overstepping. I'm perfectly capable—"

"—of taking care of yourself." He grabbed her wrist. "Yeah, I know. You've told me. Repeatedly."

She jerked her hand free and folded her arms under her breasts. "I meant I'm capable of asking for what I need."

"Doesn't appear that way to me," he snapped back, finding out he was pissed, too. He was working his ass off to help her, and she was giving him hell.

"Just because I didn't go running home to my family doesn't mean I can't accept help—the right kind of help." She shook her head. "And you're one to talk about reaching out to others, living your solitary life, dodging your family's calls. Why is it okay for you to be the only one who needs independence?"

"Whoa, whoa, whoa, let's dial this down a notch." When did this become about him? The last thing he wanted was anyone poking around inside his head or his life. "I'm trying to help. So I screwed up and didn't get it right. I'm trying."

She looked skyward, dragging in ragged breaths for thirty seconds before leveling a steely, strong gaze at him. "You may say it's not about Kevin, but I'm not so sure. Even you said on the first day back you're trying to be a stand-in dad. I get that. But it's not that simple." She held up a hand, backing away. "I've changed since last year. My life and my priorities have changed. Last night you were kissing the old Gabrielle. You don't even know the woman I am now."

Spinning away, she ran back into the house, leaving him floored.

And crazy turned on by the vibrant woman he was finding it tougher and tougher to remember had ever been engaged to his best friend.

How had she gone from totally turned on by Hank to totally furious with him in such a short time?

Gabrielle closed her computer for the workday and flopped back in the chair. Concentrating on business web designs—on anything—had been difficult with this morning's argument churning through her mind. She'd already been riding an emotional roller coaster since she lost Kevin, but now that Hank had come to town, it felt like she was stuck in a frightening loop without time for her stomach to settle.

Guilt pinched her over how she'd lost her temper with Hank. She still felt he'd gone too far in arranging care for her son without consulting her, but she wished she'd been calmer in relaying her point. He'd just hit such a sore spot with her, given the way her mom had micro-managed her life for so many years. She'd had to move an entire ocean away just to go to college without her mother checking in with her professors.

Although she had to confess, having the extra help from Leonie had been a real godsend today. She'd only asked Leonie to watch over Max while he slept, but just knowing she didn't need to keep her ears on alert, and having Leonie bring Max to her when he woke, had given Gabrielle longer stretches to catch up on business and school. She was actually—finally—back on schedule again.

Hank had steered clear of her all day, as well. Not that she could blame him. She'd seen his SUV leave shortly after their argument. Of course, he didn't have to check in with her. Still, she wondered where he'd gone. Had she actually scared him off for good? She couldn't fathom that he would just leave without saying goodbye, not matter how loudly she yelled. He wasn't that kind of man.

Which led her to the question, what kind of man was Hank Renshaw, Jr.? Besides her former fiancé's best friend. Beyond the pedigree. Beneath the uniform.

He was a good man who was trying hard to help her and her son when they weren't his responsibility. He was using his time off after a war deployment to hold her hand during her son's surgery. He was looking for ways to make her life easier, and sure, he'd bypassed her on the decision making, but she shouldn't expect him to understand parenting when he'd never been a parent.

Now that her temper had cooled, she had to admit she owed him an apology.

She shoved her chair away from the makeshift office she'd set up in her bedroom and crossed to the open nursery door. "Leonie?"

Her older neighbor—a treasured friend—looked up from her tabloid magazine as she sat curled in the daybed built into the window seat. "Yes, dear?" She set aside her gossip rag and a plate with a half-eaten sandwich. "What can I do for you and please don't say 'nothing.' I've barely done anything all day, and I'm going to feel guilty taking that generous paycheck your hot major is offering me."

"How generous?" she asked, wondering how in the world she would repay him.

"Sinfully generous, dear, and he was a total doll about the offer. Said he was doing his bit to help the economy."

Gabrielle rolled her eyes, turning away and checking on her son asleep in his bed. Seeing him sleep so peacefully, so much more content as he kept his food down better these days, warmed her soul. She had so much to be thankful for and instead she'd been stomping her foot and pitching a fit.

Leonie cleared her throat. "He drove back in about an hour ago."

Gabrielle didn't bother asking who Leonie meant. "I didn't see that."

"Ah, so you were watching out the window." She padded softly across the room and stopped by Gabrielle, covering her hand on the crib railing. "Go enjoy the rest of the evening. I have this. Really. I slept most of the day away and what little time I was awake, I was thoroughly enjoying this amazing home."

"Thank you, Leonie."

"For what?"

"For loving my son."

The older woman patted Gabrielle's cheek. "I love you, too. Now go play. Enjoy being young."

"Thanks again." Gabrielle pressed a quick kiss to her son's forehead and turned toward the hall door.

"Gabrielle, sweetie? Freshen up."

She looked down at her wrinkled T-shirt and torn jeans, coffee stains dotting them. It would be fun to dress up, to have time to do more than scrape back her hair in a hair tie. Smiling, she raced toward the connecting door back into her room and yanked open her small suitcase. Not much to pick from, but clean beat coffee-stained any day of the week.

Fifteen minutes later, she felt more like her old self in a black mini dress with red leggings, her hair loose around her shoulders. Each teasing brush along her neck reminded her of her dreams of Hank.

Was she apologizing so she could have those fantasies back and maybe bring them to life? Possibly. She wasn't sure. But she did know that for the first time in a year, she was truly…hopeful.

Her fingers trailed down the polished mahogany banister as she made her way downstairs, the sound of banging pots in the kitchen drawing her feet toward the back of the house. Standing at the six-burner gas cooktop built into the island, Hank lifted lids and stirred, three different pots going at once. A white apron splattered with red sauce looked delightfully incongruous on his hulking body. A lacy little hand towel was draped over his shoulder. An arm's reach away, he snuck bites from a serving tray with fat strawberries, soft white cheese and crostinis. Savory scents of something Italian filled the air until she salivated for everything in the room, the food and the man.

Tasting some kind of red sauce, Hank looked over the spoon at her. "Before you lose your cool, I'm cooking for me, not for you."

"Oh, really?"

"Yep, wouldn't want you to think I'm steamrolling you or anything." He dropped the spoon into the porcelain sink.

"You can call off the guards. I come in peace." She leaned against the door frame, and yeah, she relished every second of the way his eyes were drawn to her legs. The tingle of feminine power felt good, really good.

But first things first.

"Hank, I'm sorry for yelling at you earlier. I stand by what I said, but not the way I said it."

"Fair enough." He placed the lids back on the simmering pots of whatever aromatic magnificence they held. "And I apologize for not consulting you."

"You were right that I would have turned you down," she conceded with a grace he deserved.

He tugged the little towel from his shoulder and dried his hands, the island still looming between them. "And you were right. Perhaps springing the surprise on you during Max's first night home from the hospital wasn't the best timing."

"You're forgiven."

Something unsettling flickered in his cobalt-blue eyes, so fast there and gone it barely registered. "I take that to mean you're not packing."

"Staying here is best for Max." And was it best for her? It certainly shook her from her safe little routine.

Could she indulge in a no-strings affair with Hank? To hell with how different her life was now. What did it matter if this was just short-term? Even considering it made her tingle all over with the possibilities, what tonight might hold.

She shoved away from the door frame and crossed to the granite-topped island. "I'll admit, I'm frustrated that I can't give him everything he needs, but I recognize that a hotel and a worn-out mom may not be in his best interest."

He tossed the wadded towel from hand to hand. "Does that mean Leonie can stay, as well?"

"She needs the money." She circled around to him.

"And you need the help?"

"Don't push your luck." She snatched the hand towel from him in midair and snapped his hip.

He stepped closer, the air simmering between them as tangibly as the food in those pots. "I certainly don't want to blow my chances of getting lucky."

Her mouth fell open in shock. Before she could close it, Hank popped a plump strawberry between her lips. As she bit down, the explosion of flavor on her already heightened senses made her a strawberry fan for life. Life felt sharper, crisper—better—with Hank around.

She shifted her attention to the platter to give herself time to pull her thoughts together. "I'm guessing this is supper?"

"A late one, yes."

The way he said those last words felt layered somehow with a deeper meaning. But then, maybe she was searching for things she wanted to be true. "I'm here, and starving. I'm glad you waited."

Hank watched Gabrielle across the table from him, their lanai dinners becoming a habit. A very pleasurable habit. He'd spent the afternoon pulling this together for her, hoping to make up for their fight. Lights hung from the trees, like the party next door from last night. He'd cued up music, classical, like the concerts he remembered Kevin talk about attending with her and how he'd sworn his ears were bleeding by intermission.

Hank's smile faded as he looked across the table.

She was right about how it always seemed to come back to the three of them. Tonight, he needed to make this memory about just the two of them, damn it. If he couldn't do that, then he needed to walk away clean rather than tormenting them both.

He was still grateful as hell she'd forgiven him and agreed to eat supper. She'd even seemed to genuinely enjoy his homemade tomato basil sauce. His repertoire of meals wasn't that huge, but since spending a ton of money on help for her hadn't gone so well for him, he decided to opt for something more personal. She'd grown up in a family of more modest means, so he figured he might gain more traction in showing her how he'd come from a more down-to-earth family than their current media status would indicate.

She swirled her spoon through the dessert, a simple bowl of lemon sorbet. Baking a dessert stretched beyond his cooking talents.

"More?" he asked.

Groaning, she set her spoon aside. "I'm stuffed. Really. You went above and beyond, and you're making me feel guilty."

"You've been so focused on Max—and I can understand why—it seemed to me that you could use some extra TLC, as well."

"Well, you've certainly put together an amazing evening." She toyed with the hurricane globe in the middle of the table. "Who knew you're such a great cook and entertainer?"

"My sisters and I took turns setting the table. As for the minimal decorations—" he tapped the globe, with beads and a couple of Mardi Gras masks beside it "—blew over into the yard from the neighbor's party last night."

"Who would have thought a millionaire could be so thrifty."

It was billionaire, actually, but pointing that out was more likely to send her running rather than draw her in. Knowing that about her, actually drew *him* in. "My family didn't start out with all this. My dad was a regular guy, serving in the military. He earned his way through the ranks."

"You must be very proud of him."

Her comment startled him. People so often asked what his old man thought of him. Nobody turned that question around. "I am, actually. He's an amazing guy. When he was a squadron commander in Guam—"

"Guam? You lived in Guam?"

"Awesome place, like Hawaii but without a crazy crush of tourists." He preferred to remember it that way, not to think about darker times for his family after his mother died. "I'd like to take you there sometime."

"Sounds like you miss the old days, when things were simpler for your family."

Another insightful comment from the hot chick across the table, the one who totally ignored his comment about taking a trip together. He was flying into dangerous territory here, talking about his past. Lots of painful memories just waiting to shoot him down. But if he wanted to get further with Gabrielle—and he did—then he needed to suit up and soar right in.

"Life was easier before, without question."

"When did it all change?" She toyed with a feathered mask tangled up in purple beads.

He cocked his head to the side. "Are you sure you're not related to Sigmund Freud? You are half German, after all."

She swept up the mask and placed it over her eyes. "I am a woman of mystery."

Her smile sent a bolt of desire straight through him. Even if being with her could only lead to a crash and burn, he wanted her. Bad.

The mask fell away and her smile turned sheepish. "But no, I'm not Freudian, just curious about who you are. You keep so many walls up. I'm only just realizing how much you let Kevin do the talking."

"What do you want to know?"

"When did things change for you, growing up? What made you go from admiring your dad to keeping your distance?"

Pinpointing one specific event was tougher than he

would have thought. "In stages. My mom's death certainly shifted the whole family dynamic. She was a real
rock for our family during all those moves. While I say
she was a rock, she was actually the most flexible, lighthearted person in the family."

She touched his hand lightly. "What was her name?"

"Jessica. The world thinks of my dad and Ginger as a
couple, and honest to God, I don't begrudge them what
they've found together." He stared into the flame until
the world blurred. "My mom gets lost in the mix. No one
remembers her."

"Your parents had a good marriage, then?"

"I don't remember a lot, actually. I remember my mom
was the only person I ever saw stand up to my huge father.
My oldest sister said they would argue loud enough to
rattle the windows, then make up just as fast."

Next thing they knew, his mom was clearing the house
of the kids, passing his sister Alicia money to take him
and Darcy to the corner mart for soda and a candy bar.
And take your time, kiddos, his mother had said, wink-
ing back at their dad.

God, that seemed like a world ago. Alicia grew up to
fly fighter jets. She had earned a Silver Star and Dis-
tinguished Flying Cross. Little Darcy flew cargo planes
around the world.

"When I was in elementary school, Mom died a couple
of weeks after Christmas, a fluky aneurysm. No one
could have seen it coming. Some said it was a blessing
she didn't know."

"It must have been tough for you, though, not having
the chance to say goodbye."

"Sure." Except he'd been there to say goodbye to Kevin
and it hadn't made things a damn bit easier.

Hank raked up beads from the table and twisted them

around his fingers like he did when his sister Darcy made him play cat's cradle. He would have done anything for his sister after what she'd been through when they lived in Guam....

"My dad's notoriety wasn't tied into money or being married to Ginger. He gained attention for who he was. We all did." He worked the beads, passing them over his fingers by rote. "When we lived in Guam, my sister Darcy was kidnapped."

Gabrielle set the mask on the table and went completely still, her whole attention focused on him. It seemed even the night bugs went quieter, the traffic on the street fading away.

"An extremist group that wanted the military base gone from the island took her, grabbed her during a squadron family luau." From him. "They kept her for a week. She wasn't assaulted—thank God—but something like that marks a person."

"It marks a family, I imagine."

He let the beads slither from his hands. "I'm not sure why I'm telling you all of this."

"Because I asked." She slid from her chair to kneel in front of him, the feathery mask still clasped in her hand. "I'm wondering why I never asked in the year we knew each other."

He tapped her forehead. "Turn off the analysis, Dr. Freud. There's no hidden meaning here." He slipped the mask from her hand and tucked it in his shirt pocket. "Just facts."

Clasping his wrist, she pulled his hand down, kissed his palm, then pressed it to her cheek. "Facts that explain to me how it could be scary as hell for you to let a woman get too close to y—"

He hauled her up by her elbows and kissed her silent.

It was one thing to fly into the painful midst of his past. It was a whole other matter to have Gabrielle peel away any defenses he had left.

Her lips parted without hesitation, the lingering taste of lemon sorbet on her tongue. He pulled her onto his lap, his hands finally, finally touching her, roving over her back, grazing the side of her lush breasts. He skimmed down her waist and over her hips. He'd waited so long to touch her, he soaked up every detail. The hem of her mini dress bunched in his hands and next thing he knew he was touching bare flesh above the waistline of her leggings.

She thrust her fingers in his hair, pulling him closer, not protesting one damn bit. Heat seared him inside and out. This attraction was no figment of anyone's imagination, no faulty memory. This was real and intense.

And about to become more so.

Eight

Moving from the lanai to Hank's bedroom passed in a blur of kissing, touching and frantic hands exploring as they climbed the steps and sealed themselves away from the world.

The door clicked shut, nestling them in the privacy of his bedroom.

Gabrielle pressed closer to Hank, couldn't get near enough after so long of wanting to touch him, to explore the hard muscled planes of his body. She'd been trying to hold back from this ache for so long, and now she could finally have him. If only for tonight or whatever time he had left in New Orleans, she could finally surrender to the tenacious passion that tugged at them.

Her leg hooked around his, her foot stroking his calf. The scent of oregano and thoughtfulness clung to him. The home-cooked food, the lighted trees and table decorations all put together by him touched her more than any catered meal.

He nuzzled her ear, his breath almost as hot as her tingling flesh. "Are you sure this isn't moving too fast for you?"

She gasped for breath, her pulse throbbing in her chest...and lower. "The way I kissed you last night didn't clue you in?"

"I was hopeful, but there's no timetable here, no rush," he vowed against her hair, stroking her neck, her shoulders, cupping her breasts in hands both bold and gentle at once.

"We've both been waiting a long time for this." Even hinting at the past, at the conflicting feelings of a year ago chilled her, threatening to steal away this beautiful moment. "Let's focus on here and now."

His arms slid around her, steely bands of strength. "I always knew you were a brilliant woman."

She kissed along the bristly texture of his jaw up to his ear. "This whole night has been amazing."

"I hope it's about to get even better." He tunneled up her mini dress, thumbs hooking in the band of her leggings.

A delicious shiver slid over her at the feel of his touch on her bare skin.

"I would say that's a safe guess." Her head fell back, giving him free access to her neck.

His hands cupped new curves, lingering with infinite tenderness and appreciation. He made her feel beautiful and sexy, all the more special in the wake of having been pregnant. She reveled in the feel of his hard thighs pressed to her, his hips tight against hers.

He nudged aside the collar of her dress with his chin and nibbled along her shoulder, sending wisps of pleasure over her skin. "We need to move to the bed or this is going to happen against the door."

"Is the door so wrong?" She tugged his chambray shirt from his khaki waistband and tucked her fingers in to urge him closer.

"Not at all—" he kissed upward until he looked in her eyes again "—except I've waited for you too long to rush."

His voice rumbled with promise. He clasped hands with her and walked backward toward the looming mahogany four-poster bed. The rest of the room came into focus for the first time.

Seeing his sparse room made her realize just how much trouble he'd gone to for her and for Max. The spacious master suite contained only the bed, a massive armoire, since there were no closets in the historic home, and two wingback chairs by the fireplace. The space was as stark as the man, a wealthy frame but Spartan in presentation.

Her legs bumped the back of the mattress. She was really going to do this, steal a night with Hank. Nerves and anticipation mixed into an intoxicating swirl flooding her veins. Her fingers sped down the buttons of his shirt. She whipped the fabric from his shoulders and flung it aside, the feathery mask sailing out of the pocket.

She'd seen him in swim trunks before, but this was so very different, so intimate. She allowed herself the pleasure of just looking at him, taking in the thick column of his neck, his sculpted chest honed from the sun and exercise.

A scar grazed his collarbone.

Frowning, she traced the inch-long pucker of scar tissue. "What happened here?"

"Shrapnel." He dismissed her question, clasping her

hand and kissing her wrist, taking his time along her racing pulse. "Nothing big."

Nothing big? The scar looked deep and close to his jugular vein. An inch over and she would have lost him, too. One heartbeat tripped over another before settling back into a regular rhythm.

Could this have happened when Kevin was killed? The thought threatened to ice her from the inside out.

Hank bracketed her face with his hands. "Stop thinking about it. That's the past. Come back to living in the moment."

His thumbs stroked her cheeks until she hooked her arms around his waist. "Make me forget, Hank, please."

"I can't think of anything I want more." He slanted his mouth over hers again, his mouth warm and familiar now.

His bold, confident hands bunched her dress up— breaking the kiss for only a second—and swept the clothing over her head. His eyes turned blue-flame hot as he nipped his way down her body, between her breasts, further down to peel off her leggings, his mouth following his hands. Kneeling in front of her, he tossed her pants into the growing pile of their clothes.

She hadn't been with anyone since Kevin—since having a baby—and her body was different now. She didn't consider herself shallow or overly vain. But this was her first time with stretch marks and an extra few pounds. Her mouth went dry.

Hank's eyes filled with admiration, grasping her hips with a low growl of approval. "You are even more beautiful than I imagined. And believe me, I have imagined you this way more times that I can count."

His hand stroked up again, holding...

She looked down. He'd picked up the feathered Mardi Gras mask, trailing in a silky teasing path, along her leg, over her hip and higher until he stood in front of her again.

Already gasping in anticipation, she made fast work of his belt, his zipper, until he kicked away his khakis and boxers. She grazed her fingers down the ridged six-pack of his stomach, to his narrow hips, sliding over to encircle his erection, which strained upward against his belly. Slowly, she caressed him, stroked him, working her thumb over the pearly bead on top, slicking her hand. Watching his face, the way he bit his bottom lip, sent a rush straight through her.

His jaw flexed with tension, his eyes sliding closed for two heartbeats before he clasped her wrist and drew her hand away. In a flash, he bracketed her waist and tossed her gently on the bed.

Climbing up the bed, he stretched over her, large and restrained all at once. And in his hand, he still held the Mardi Gras mask. He stroked the feathers along her neck with just the right amount of pressure to tantalize without tickling. Hmm…that felt so unexpected and good.

Her head lolled to the side and thank goodness he got the message to continue along her collar bone, back and forth until goose bumps rose along her skin. He trailed the silky softness between her breasts, circling one then the other, again and again, until she bit her bottom lip to keep from crying out at the tingling pleasure, to keep from begging him for more.

He flicked one taut nipple, then the other. Back and forth, he drew patterns of pleasure along her skin while she murmured a mix of pleas and demands. She gripped his arm, her head pressing back into the pillow.

The feather skimmed along her stomach, then around to the inside of her thighs, so close to teasing where she needed him most. She gasped for air—for release—her pulse thundering in her ears.

His fingers replaced the feathers. Then his mouth. Her hands went to his shoulders, holding him in place. Taking her pleasure. Her mind filled with all the ways she would please him through the night.

The flick of his tongue, the sweet subtlety of his touch drove her higher. Then she couldn't think about anything but the velvet feel of how he gave and gave to her, taking her so close—

But she didn't want to go alone. He'd already done so much for her. She needed them to be partners in this much as least.

"Hank," she gasped, drawing him upward until he stretched over her again. "Now. I want all of you now."

She arched her hips against him, the thick length of him pressing against her. If she moved, adjusted, angled him, she could have him inside her, flesh to flesh—

Oh, God! Her nails dug into his shoulders. "Condoms... How could I have forgotten?"

She wouldn't trade Max for anything in the world, but the pregnancy had been an accident, the product of a night when she and Kevin had too much to drink and got sloppy about using birth control.

"You didn't forget because you just spoke up—" he cupped her face "—and I have that taken care of."

Rolling to his side, he reached to the bedside table and opened a drawer. The box was still sealed, and she realized he'd bought the condoms for this, for *them*.

She angled up on her elbows, watching as he sheathed himself. Anticipation, and more of those nerves pattering through her. So she looped her arms around his neck and drew him to her, needing the forgetfulness she was damn certain she could find with him. The thick pressure between her thighs chased away any doubts.

Hooking her legs around his, she urged him on, welcomed him inside her until he was heart deep. Her eyes squeezed closed to battle back emotional tears because finally she had him, after so long wondering and wanting, and the feel of him moving inside her was even more than she'd anticipated. And yes, even more than she'd feared because something this special made her rethink the rest of her life.

Although the last thing she wanted to do right now was make plans for the future. She wanted to live in the moment, just the two of them, the scent of her lavender soap mixing with his aftershave. The special blend of *them* clung to the air. She rolled her hips as Hank thrust, their bodies syncing into a rhythm unique to the two of them.

The sound of his voice in her ear stoked her along with the slick glide of their bare bodies against each other. So close, he took her to the edge again and again, holding back at the last second until she clawed at his back, desperate for release until—

Wave after wave crested over her, shattering her with the intensity of bliss restrained for far too long. A cry rolled up her throat, and he captured the sound with his mouth—or maybe he was muffling the hoarse shout of his own release.

His arms folded, and he blanketed her. Aftershocks trembled through her, through him, as well, binding them all over again.

Slowly, awareness returned, bit by bit with the cool gusts of air from a ceiling fan she hadn't even noticed before. Her hands roved over Hank's body, a precious weight anchoring her to the bed. Somehow, the mask had been crushed between them, but she couldn't bring herself to make him move so she could toss it aside.

For now, the masks were off literally and symbolically. No past or future casting shadows.

Right now, she had Hank in her arms, and she held on tight, scared as hell of how badly it would hurt to lose him if she let herself care too much. Having had her heart shattered once, she wasn't sure she had the strength to risk experiencing that pain a second time.

Hank sprawled naked on his bed, working to catch his breath after round two with Gabrielle. She'd proved to be equally as adept in playing with the mask and tormenting the hell out of him.

Then satisfying the hell out of him.

Being with her had been every bit as world-rocking as he'd expected. Now he just had to work to make sure she didn't run scared. Because already he could see doubts and fears chasing through her eyes.

Curled up beside him, which also kept her face averted, she toyed with the feathered mask. "I hadn't pegged you for the playful type, but I like the surprise."

"Glad to hear it." He stroked his knuckles along the small of her back, just above the sweet curve of her bottom.

"You're different here, away from the squadron, more open."

His father's shadow wasn't lurking around each corner ready to ambush him here. "Everyone wears a facade at some point."

"Being bare is a scary thing, being vulnerable." She shivered and he tugged the satin comforter over her.

He tucked the covers around her and pulled her back to his side. "I'm not going to hurt you."

A choked laugh sputtered from her. "No one can promise that. Life hurts."

He knuckled her chin upward until she had to look in his eyes again. "Are you hurting right now?"

She shook her head. "No, of course not. I'm happy and satiated and a little scared, but not sad. Not hurting."

"Good...very good." He dipped his head and kissed her, lingering until she sighed. "Let's see if we can keep you that way. I have a gift for you."

"Another one?" She crinkled her nose. "You're going to have to get your business partner to invent a new game if you keep this up."

"Trust me." He saw the uneasiness in her eyes, the fear that he would give her something totally inappropriate after they'd had sex. She really didn't know him well at all. But he intended to change that.

He padded across the bedroom floor to the mammoth wardrobe and pulled out a gift bag from a French Quarter *parfumeur.* Her eyebrows pinched together curiously as she tucked the Egyptian cotton sheet under her arms. He dropped the bag into the middle of the bed where it landed with a hefty *thump.*

Tugging out red-and-gold tissue paper and tossing it onto the bed, she peered inside the gold foil bag. A slow smile spread across her face....

"Bubble bath!" she squealed, pulling out one bottle, then the next, digging her way through the bag filled with different scents and bathing accessories with obvious joy.

"You'd mentioned hurried showers before now. There are definite perks to having me and a nanny around. You can stay in the tub as long as you like."

She uncorked a small bottle of scented oil and sniffed, moaning in ecstasy. "Heaven."

Chuckling, he passed her a long skinny box. He had

definite ideas for that oil later. "I know this isn't as nice as diamonds, but I figured you would pitch jewels back in my lap anyway."

"You figured right. Besides, bath pearls are more precious than the real kind because this really was thoughtful."

"So why don't you go try it out now?"

"Right now?"

"Sure. The bathroom's right through there."

She rocked forward on her knees and kissed him fast before gathering up her French milled soaps and gels and whatever else chicks called the rest of the stuff. Nearly tripping over the sheet in her excitement, she raced straight for the master bath.

Hank sat in the middle of the bed, leaning back against the headboard and listening to her hum as she filled the tub. As much as he wanted to have her again, he wasn't going to interrupt her first long bath since her son had been born.

How insane was it that he felt every bit as good about sitting here listening to her sing as he had when making love to her? The sound of her voice stroked him just as completely as her hands.

Damn. Gabrielle might be the one in the tub, but he was the one in serious hot water.

Now that he'd had her, there was no way in hell he could let her go.

Gabrielle toed the hot water on again, reheating the tub for the third time.

There had to be a special place in heaven for whoever invented the tankless water heater. This hour-long bath soaked stress from parts of her body she hadn't even realized were kinked. Tension slipped from her every time she opened the drain.

Although she couldn't give all the credit to the spa bath. Lavender perfume hung in the humid air, Hank's thoughtful gifts soothing her soul and tugging her heart all at once. The man could have bought her jewels, which she wouldn't have accepted. Or chocolates, which she couldn't eat because of nursing Max.

Instead, Hank had paid attention to her needs, to the scent she wore.

She sank deeper into the tub big enough for two and soaked in the mellow tan and butter cream-colored decor around her. Maybe she would finish off with a shower, another pure spa delight with jets lining the corners to spray from all angles.

There was even a flat-screen television mounted high in a corner if she wanted to lean back, hide out and watch a movie.

This place was mama nirvana. She'd never considered herself a materialistic person, but she wouldn't mind having this all to herself at the end of each day.

With Hank waiting for her in the bedroom?

She couldn't ignore that they'd taken a huge step tonight. As much as she wanted to tell herself it was only a fling, she wasn't an affair kind of person. She was still the same person she'd been from the start—the girl who'd lived to be a mother, to have her own happily ever after with the best dressed, most well fed, happiest babies on the block.

Which brought her right back to those fears that had iced her after making love to Hank.

Her last romantic relationship hadn't gone all that great, even before Kevin died. That last fight with him kept whispering through her mind, how he'd wanted her to move near him and she'd resisted.

Was she crazy to be thinking of the future now? If anything, Hank was more tied to the military lifestyle than Kevin had been. As if their shared past with Kevin didn't already make things complicated enough.

She toed the hot water off. There wasn't a heater big enough to chase away the chill settling into her bones.

Listening to Gabrielle take a bath had been pure torture. But as much as he wanted to slide into the water with her and make love to every inch of her body, he was determined to let her have her quiet time alone, soaking.

Pivoting away from temptation, he pulled on sweat pants, left his room and headed for hers. He could check on Max, give Leonie a break if she was awake. Seemed as if the entire household had an upside down sleeping schedule, their lives wrapped up in making sure Max was okay.

As it should be.

He stepped into her room, scanning for where she'd left the nursery monitor. Leonie's voice crooned from the next room as she sang some old nursery rhyme. A memory flashed of his mom singing off-key while she decorated the tree, his dad hooking an arm around her waist and vowing his ears were bleeding from the sound.

Both of them laughing together.

Everyone told him she'd been a great mom and from the videos he'd seen, they were right. His dad hadn't talked about her much over the years, just saying she'd been a real wonder woman, parenting alone most of the time since the military lifestyle kept him away.

Hank trailed a finger along the edge of Gabrielle's makeshift workstation. She'd set up her laptop on the sofa

table behind the love seat and pulled a chair from the hall
to set up a mini-office. For her website work? Or school?
Or both while she took care of her son? She carried the
load of three women. He dropped into the seat and wished
somehow he could absorb some of the burden for her.

His eyes landed on two scrapbooks resting on a stack
of her textbooks. He pulled the album off the top and
thumbed it open.

Kevin's face stared back at him like a sucker punch
from the grave.

Hank studied the photo of Kevin with Gabrielle at the
squadron Christmas ball, a red rosebud pressed to the
corner of the image like a splash of blood. The staged
portrait didn't tell him much other than that it commemo-
rated an event. He flipped the page and found a photo of
the three of them at a Shreveport Captains baseball game.
Gabrielle wore a jersey and cap, her blond ponytail lifted
by the wind. Kevin had his arm hooked around her shoulders. They appeared happy. Really happy.

He looked at himself…and crap.

No wonder Kevin knew how he felt about Gabrielle.
One look at this picture would have told an idiot that
Hank had a thing for her. His eyes were glued to her like
a starving guy on food after a hunger strike.

Yet Gabrielle hadn't picked up on it. She'd seemed
stunned when he'd kissed her a year ago. Or she'd kissed
him, as she kept insisting. Once they started, it had been
mutual.

Would he ever get over feeling guilty? Even now, the
weight of it bored into him like eyes watching him from
the grave.

He glanced up fast. Gabrielle stood in the open doorway wearing a simple satin robe. The fabric clung to
her damp body in places, her face still flushed from the

steamy heat. Her hair was piled up on her head, wisps trailing down and sticking to her neck. Just the sight of her had him wanting her again. His hand fisted on top of the photo.

She walked deeper into the room and sat on the love seat, resting her chin on her arms and staring at him over the sofa back. "I thought you might come join me in the tub."

"I thought the bath was about you having time to yourself. If I joined you, doesn't that negate the whole alone-time point?"

"That's actually a very intuitive thought."

"For a guy, you mean?" He faked a smile. "Hey, call me Joe Sensitive."

"You mean Major Joe Sensitive, right?" She laughed, but something sounded off. "I did enjoy the long soak. I may have even drifted off."

"Good."

Her eyes settled on the scrapbook in front of him.

He closed the album, fast. "I shouldn't have looked without asking you."

She reached to open the book again and turned it toward her. "It's silly to keep one of these and then never let anyone look at it. I'm sorry that seeing pictures of him upset you."

"Actually…" He flipped it to the page in question. "I was more upset with myself."

"I'm not sure I follow."

He tapped the edge of the ballgame photo. "Could I have been any more obvious?"

"I didn't know." Her hand gravitated to his face in the picture, tracing his jaw until he could almost feel her phantom touch. "I mean, I knew that I was attracted to you. But I didn't know you felt the same and especially not on a long-term basis."

"The way I kissed you didn't tip you off?"

"I figured I threw myself at you. You reacted on impulse. Which doubled my guilty feelings because I worried I might have harmed your friendship with Kevin."

"Impulse, like hell." He leaned back, folding his hands over his stomach. "Suppressed frustration's more like it."

She slid from the sofa and walked around to sit on the arm of his chair. Her fingers sketched his jaw for real, her fingertips soft and scented from her bath. "We have about a week and a half left to work those out."

A week and a half and then he returned to base, to work.

And she stayed in New Orleans?

She hadn't been willing to move for Kevin. She sure as hell wasn't going to move because they had one night of crazy hot sex between them. He needed to use his time wisely to persuade her they'd started something here. Guilt be damned, he couldn't let her go.

He pulled her into his lap and nipped her ear. "What do you say I carry you back to my room?"

"I think you should carry me back to that spa tub so I can take another bath—with you."

Nine

Getting used to sharing a bed again was easier said than done. Especially since Hank was a serious covers hog.

Yawning, she struggled to orient herself, having been tugged from a deep sleep by the abrupt rush of air over her body. Gabrielle patted the bed in the dark, searching for a corner of the bedspread to yank.

In the week since they'd started sharing a bed—after amazing sex—she'd fast learned that he was a restless sleeper. Which was only made worse by the fact that she was a light sleeper after so many months keeping her ears tuned in for the smallest sound from her son.

But there were so many good things to offset Hank's cover-snatching habit. Their week together had been packed with more great food and amazing sex. They'd even gone on outings with Max, a long drive, a simple walk along Lake Ponchartrain with Max in the stroller, a concert in the park. People mistook them for a family.

They felt like a family.

She blinked to adjust her eyes, but it was still dark. Moonlight streamed through the dormer window, slashing a pale yellow streak across the bed. She rolled to locate even a sheet and found Hank sitting up.

His eyes were open, but he was clearly still asleep. He'd tossed the covers to the ground. His fists were twisted in the fitted sheet. His mouth moved, mumbling something unintelligible, as if he couldn't force the sound out.

He was in the middle of a nightmare. A really bad one, gauging by the tendons standing out along his neck. Pain, fear and something very dark pulsed from Hank like waves off a toxic cloud.

How could she wake him up without startling him?

She was afraid to touch him. Not that she thought he would ever deliberately hurt her, but he looked ready to snap. A simple touch could make him lash out.

Leaning away slowly, she turned on the lamp, hoping that might ease him out of whatever night terrors gripped him. His head twitched, but still he didn't wake. Words tumbled from his mouth, some taking shape, others not so much.

Look out. God. No. Kevin. Hold on.

Realization seeped through her, that toxic cloud expanding to draw her in, as well. Hank was dreaming of Kevin's death.

Her chest went tight. She wanted to yank on her robe and run far, far away. But she couldn't leave him in that hell alone. He'd already lived through it once, a torture no one should face. Ever.

"Hank," she said softly but firmly. "Wake up. You're in New Orleans with me. Gabrielle. You're all right. It's just a dream. Can you hear me?"

Blinking faster, he hauled in breath after breath until he turned to her. "Gabrielle?"

She rested just her fingertips on his arm. "Are you okay?"

He scrubbed both hands over his head. "Crap. No." His voice came out raw and ragged, as if he was pushing the words over broken glass. "Just give me a second."

"You were dreaming about being in the Middle East, weren't you?"

He nodded without speaking.

"About Kevin?"

He nodded again, pulling away to sit on the edge of the bed. If she let the silence stretch, he would leave. His feet were already on the floor. He would shut her out and deal with the pain on his own.

After all he'd done for her, she couldn't let him shoulder everything. The man put up hefty walls. Time for somebody to be persistent enough to scale them.

She scooted to sit behind him, leaning her cheek on his shoulder blade. "Seeing Max and me must bring it all back. This can't be what the military meant by taking time off to recharge after a deployment." She stroked his arm, up and down, again and again, until the tensed muscles relaxed. "Maybe it would have been better for you if you hadn't come here right away."

"Don't go blaming yourself." He grabbed her hand fiercely. "I could look at a damn penny and somehow it would make me think of Kevin and that day...."

"Can you tell me what happened?" she asked, only half sure she really wanted to know, but she couldn't bail on Hank now.

He glanced back at her, the moonlight casting stark shadows on his face. "Didn't Kevin's parents tell you? They were given the official report."

"I know what happened to him and that you were there." Although they hadn't been overly wordy in sharing the details. To this day, she was foggy on why he'd been attacked on the ground. She'd always expected that if the worst happened, it would come from their plane being shot down. Bile burned as she thought about losing both Kevin and Hank. "I want to hear what happened to *you*."

He stayed silent so long she feared he might not talk, after all.

Then a sigh racked through him. "We were at a checkpoint. Everyone had to get out of the bus and show papers. Should have been quick and easy, wasn't even particularly a hot zone."

His heart hammered faster under her ear as she kept her cheek pressed to his back. She slid her arms around him, holding him, and yes, making sure he didn't bolt away. She just held him and waited.

"A sniper hit Kevin with two shots before I could even move to cover him."

Only a few simple words, and he'd transported her there with the pain in his voice. She could almost smell the acrid air, feel the grit of sand in her mouth because she would have screamed. God, how could anyone not?

"I carried Kevin back to the bus."

She hugged Hank tighter, the ridge of scar tissue on his collarbone suddenly all the more awful. "Is that when you got the scar?"

"Yeah."

She squeezed her eyes closed, swallowed down the push of tears. He had been shot, too. She could have lost them both. But right now was about Hank, being there for him the way he'd been there for her.

Clearing his throat, he continued, "Back in the truck,

I radioed for the medics to backtrack, but the frequency was full of everyone calling in. I tore off his vest, his shirt."

Her mind filled with images of those final moments of Kevin's life spent in a stark military bus in a foreign land. How many others had been on the bus with them? Just his crew or other crews, as well? She could hear the voices, the shouts, imagine the smell of death and desperation.

And Kevin's last thoughts of her had been about how he knew she and Hank had feelings for each other. Guilt blanketed her all over again. Might Kevin have found some comfort in knowing she was expecting his child? She hated that she hadn't shared the news with him. She'd thought it would distract him when he needed to focus and in the end he'd died anyway. She battled back her tears, needing to be strong for Hank.

"I'm sure you did everything you could," she offered, knowing it wasn't enough. Knowing he barely heard her since his eyes were unfocused, and, in his mind, he still knelt over Kevin in a hellish desert.

"I did the only thing I could think to." The words fell faster and faster from him. "I put my fingers in the bullet holes to try to stop the bleeding. He asked me to look after you, and then I watched the life leave his eyes."

Her heart broke at the desperation he must have felt.

Hank stood sharply, her arms falling away. He didn't look back, just grabbed his jeans from the back of a chair, hauled them on and left the room. As the door closed behind him, she realized she'd been so worried about how much being together would hurt her. She'd selfishly overlooked how much being with her must hurt him.

Even if she managed to get past the guilt to take this affair into a relationship, Hank might not.

* * *

Hank charged down the stairs to the kitchen.

He needed a beer but would settle for anything that gave him an excuse to walk out of that room full of memories. The nightmare had been bad enough, but reliving the day Kevin died drained him dry. He'd spent ten months coming to grips with what happened. But coming back to the states, being here with Gabrielle, it was as if he had to learn to deal with Kevin's death all over again.

Biting back a curse, Hank rounded the corner into the renovated kitchen and stopped short.

Leonie sat at the island eating a slice of pecan pie and thumbing through a tabloid magazine while Max snoozed away in his baby carrier. "Hello, Major." She slid from the tall swivel chair, tightening the sash on the robe over her lounging pj's. "Could I get you a plate? There's plenty left."

"No thanks. I'm good." Except actually, he wasn't "good." He was a damn mess inside and would be better off alone. He opened the refrigerator and pulled out a carton of juice. He tipped it back just like he did at *his* condo. To hell with manners. He wasn't in the mood for niceties.

"Glad to see the two of you working things out." Her fork clanked against the plate. "I wasn't too certain there at the outset."

"Why so?" He turned to face her, the carton still in his hand.

"You hired a nanny without consulting her the day her son got home from the hospital." She dabbed the corners of her mouth with her napkin. "Any woman would be upset."

"Then why did you take the job if you knew it was

going to make her mad?" He would never understand women.

"I needed the money. She needed the rest." She smiled, her hand smoothing the light blanket over Max tenderly. "And I love this little fellow."

"You could have clued me in so I didn't piss her off."

"Telling a person what to do never works, not in the long haul." She took her plate to the sink and rinsed off the crumbs. "The real lessons in life are learned from actions, making mistakes and fixing them yourself. That's the way good relationships are built."

"Relationships?" He winced.

"Please, do not be that cliché, relationship-leery man." Sighing, Leonie leaned back against the granite slab countertop. "I pegged you for better than that."

He'd just wanted something to drink, some space to pull himself back together and now he was catching it from all sides from a woman he barely knew. "Why are you giving me such a hard time?"

"Because you don't have a mama, and for some reason you don't have much contact with your family. Who else is going to tell you what you need to hear?"

He cocked an eyebrow, channeling his dad's superior look. But what the hell? He followed in the old man's footsteps just about every other way. "You've been reading too many tabloids."

"I do love my gossip papers." She grinned unrepentantly. "News about your family sells."

He spun the tabloid rag around. A headline blared, Granny Ginger Buys Princess Granddaughter a Pony. The rest of the article detailed some supposedly lavish birthday bash his stepmom had thrown for her newest grandchild—a girl whose mother was an illegitimate princess.

The guest list included everyone from the kids of movie stars to ambassadors.

Since emails from home had included details and photos from that party, he knew ninety-nine percent of the information was bull. His mom had rented a pony, but the very long guest list for the toddler's first birthday was simply all the family members. So what if the family members happened to be Renshaws, Landises and in-law royal Medinas? But apparently stuff like this, touting inside peeks into the lifestyles of the rich and famous, sold magazines.

An ugly suspicion niggled. "How badly do you need money?"

Her smile faded. "Not bad enough to ever do anything to hurt Gabrielle or this little boy, and I'll scratch out the eyes of anyone who does."

He searched her eyes and found nothing but honesty. "Good, we're on the same page, then."

"So you'll think about what I said?"

"Said about what?"

She'd said so freaking much he'd lost track.

"Men," she mumbled, reaching for Max's seat.

Hank grasped the carrier handle. "I'll take him for a while."

"It's okay, Major." Leonie patted his hand. "I've got him."

"Seriously, go nap or read a gossip magazine. It can't be easy switching to the night shift all at once."

"Okay, then." She pulled a baby rattle and empty bottle from her pocket as she spun away. "You're the boss."

He set the juice carton on the island, taking his seat in front of the sleeping baby. Kevin's kid. Gabrielle's son.

Shaking the cow-shaped rattle in front of the boy's face, he tracked the faces of both people he loved in the kid's cheeks and stubborn chin. Max blinked wide blue eyes back at him and all those features merged into one, a unique individual.

Max.

A roaring started in his ears, and he reached to pick up the baby. He cradled Max in the crook of his arm, shaking the rattle again since the boy seemed to like it. Max batted at the air, his little fist bumping Hank's, baby skin softer than anything he could remember. Tiny fingers unfurled and wrapped around his thumb, holding tight.

"Hey, buddy," he said softly, "we're going to have fun together. Do you like baseball? With a grip like that, I'll bet you can throw a mean curve ball. You and me, we're going to be…"

Be…what? He wasn't sure where he stood with the child. What would those scrapbooks show when Gabrielle added photos of him with Max? He didn't want to be a stand-in dad. He wanted to be the real thing. A father to Max and a husband to Gabrielle.

But he also didn't want to forget Kevin, and he wasn't sure how in the hell to cohabitate with a ghost.

Gabrielle woke up alone with the covers all to herself. So why wasn't she happy?

She reached to touch the empty spot beside her, and the sheets weren't even warm. Hank hadn't come back to bed after his nightmare. She'd thought getting him to talk about the dream and what happened ten months ago would make him feel better. But what did she know about war memories? She could have made things worse for him by venturing in full steam when he wasn't ready.

Where did she go from here?

Maybe she needed to stop pushing, to give him some space. Kevin had always talked about how Hank kept his distance from his family, that he was the sort of guy who liked to keep his life private. Today, he had to be especially vulnerable—although she could almost see him bristle if she called him vulnerable to his face. He wasn't one to acknowledge his own emotional needs so she would have to take care of those for him.

She could probably use a little elbow room, too. Things had happened at such a fast and furious pace—moving here, Max's surgery, starting an affair. She pressed a hand to her aching heart and wished life could be simple for a change.

Although some things were straightforward. Like her son's needs. She grabbed her robe from the corner of the bed and shrugged it on. Flicking her hair free and finger combing it, she went in search of her son for his morning feeding. She creaked open the nursery door.

Leonie sat in the window seat reading a gossip magazine. She looked up, bifocals sliding down on her nose. "Max is downstairs with the major. He insisted on watching him and who am I to argue with a hot man taking care of a baby." She fanned her face with the magazine. "*Phew.* Now that's sexy."

"Thanks for the update, Leonie." Gabrielle's heart squeezed at the thought of Hank hurting over the loss of his friend and then having that friend's child right there in front of him. But Hank, being Hank, was so busy thinking about others—letting her rest, giving Leonie a break—he put himself dead last.

Hopefully, she could feed Max quickly then go out for the morning. Take a walk with her son. Proofread a school paper in the park.

Gain some much needed distance and perspective to sort through her life.

She searched each of the bedrooms upstairs, but no Hank or Max. She took the back stairs into the kitchen, also empty other than a dish in the sink and a half-empty juice carton on the island. Her bare feet padded along the kitchen tile to the hardwood of the hall. She pinched the neck of her robe closed, wishing now that she'd taken a second to put on some clothes, or at least to put on a nightgown underneath.

Finally, she found Hank in the library. Curtains closed, the room stayed hazy with only minimal morning light shining through but it was plenty bright enough for her to see Hank. He lay stretched out asleep on the leather sofa.

Max slept on his chest.

Leonie was one smart cookie, because right now, Gabrielle couldn't think of anything more appealing than the sight of her baby napping on Hank's bare chest. His broad hand held the infant, and she didn't doubt for a second that if Max so much as wriggled, Hank would keep him safely in place.

Hiring the sitter had been a thoughtful, generous gesture. But seeing how Hank chose to hold Max, to watch over him as he slept, that nearly brought Gabrielle to her knees.

A low buzzing sound drew her attention to the end table where Hank's wallet and cell phone rested. The buzz sounded again, and she realized his cell was vibrating with an incoming call.

Hank reached over his head, grappled for the phone, and thumbed the ringer silent. He turned his head toward her, his eyes opening, blue and clear as if he'd been awake the whole time. "How long have you been standing there?"

"Only a minute or so. I need to nurse Max."

Her son stirred at the sound of her voice, stretching his tiny arms over his head and yawning. She walked toward Hank as he sat up, adjusting his hold on Max like a seasoned pro.

"Sure, here you go." He passed her boy over to her without touching her or meeting her eyes.

Silence settled between them, full of what he'd told her last night. She would have run upstairs right that second but Max wriggled in her arms, fussy and searching for food.

She sat on the end of the sofa, parting her robe and bringing her son to her breast. He squirmed, rooting frantically for a few seconds before latching on with a hungry sigh. Hank stayed on the far end of the couch, rubbing the back of his neck, looking from her to the hall and back again.

Hank's phone vibrated again, and he snatched it up, turning it off altogether before stuffing it in his back pocket. For a guy who'd been sleeping so peacefully, his mood had certainly done a serious one-eighty now that he was awake.

The minute Max finished, she was definitely going to give herself and Hank some breathing room. She would even take Leonie along with her so Hank could have the house to himself. In fact, she heard Leonie on the stairway now, which gave her the perfect out.

"Hank, I think that—"

The doorbell rang, cutting her off short. She looked up fast just as Leonie rushed the rest of the way down the stairs.

Gabrielle cupped her son's head protectively. Hank shot to his feet. Voices drifted from the hall, Leonie's along with others she didn't recognize.

She cradled her son closer. "Has someone broken into the house?"

Hank dropped back to the sofa, a curse hissing from between his tight teeth. "It's not a break-in. It's my family."

Ten

Gabrielle wanted to run. Anywhere would be fine. Just some place far away from the four adults standing with Leonie in the archway staring at her, their jaws slack with surprise. Not that she could blame them. If only she'd had some advance warning she could have dashed upstairs to dress. But the curtains were closed, and she'd been so wrapped up in Max and Hank and making sure they both were all right, she'd completely missed Hank's family's approach.

She'd read enough articles about the Renshaw and Landis families to recognize the small group. It didn't take gossip magazines to keep up with them. Hank's military general dad stood with his second wife, Ginger. A younger couple hovered behind them. While Ginger's four sons resembled each other, Gabrielle was almost certain this was the youngest, the architect who did renovations on historic homes—and also happened to be married to a woman with royal roots to her family tree. His wife jostled a toddler on her hip, a little girl around a year old.

What must they all think?

She didn't have to ask. She knew exactly what any reasonable person would assume based on the way things looked. Hank stood barefoot, particularly sexy in nothing more than a pair of jeans riding low on his hips. And she really wished that she'd put on something more than just a robe and that she was anywhere other than on the sofa nursing her son.

If she pulled Max away, she risked exposing herself to the already stunned quartet. Plus he would scream himself purple if she cut his meal short.

Were they judging her? Wondering if she was taking advantage of Hank? She wondered the same thing herself. She searched their eyes and only found curiosity.

A lot of it.

She looked to Hank for help just as he stepped toward his family.

"As you can see, we weren't expecting company. How about we step across the hall and give Gabrielle some privacy with her son? Introductions can wait until then."

He ushered them out into the hall, pulling the doors closed behind him.

Voices seeped through, lots of voices, rising with curiosity as they all must be bombarding him with questions. If only she could make out the words. Her son continued to blissfully nurse, unaware of the world turned upside down.

A few minutes later, the door opened again and Gabrielle tensed. Leonie slid through, keeping the room shielded from the rest of the house.

"Cavalry to the rescue, sweetie. I have clothes for you." She held up her hands with—thank God—something to wear. "I'm ready to take the little guy if you're about done." Leonie sat beside her, a clothing stack perched on her knees.

Max seemed to be slowing, and Gabrielle would just live with feeling lopsided rather than taking more time to swap him to the other breast. "You'll just need to burp him."

"Will do." Leonie took the baby and patted him on the back. "Can you believe we're actually under the same roof as a former secretary of state? And royalty?"

"Believe it or not, they're here, all right." Gabrielle just wished they'd called first. Her plans for giving Hank space went out the window.

Shielded by the robe, she stepped into her underwear and jeans, then shrugged on her bra and long white poet's shirt. She shoved her feet into sandals. Dressed, thank goodness.

Maybe she would still be able to make it to her room to freshen up further. She cracked open the double doors to peek out.

No luck.

Across the hall in the dining room, Hank stood with his surprise guests. All eyes homed in on her. Leonie tucked by and took Max up the stairs, which pulled the attention off Gabrielle momentarily.

Holding her head high, Gabrielle rolled back her shoulders. Hank slid into place beside her and palmed her waist. He ducked his head and whispered, "I haven't told them anything. I wanted to wait for you to weigh in, although nobody's going to believe us if we say we're not together."

He kissed her cheek and straightened. She didn't even bother protesting. They *were* sleeping together and denying it would make a bigger deal out of the situation.

"Ginger, Dad," Hank said, "this is Gabrielle."

Hank Renshaw, Sr., nodded silently, a graying, older version of his son, and just as reticent. He didn't need the uniform to look like a general. Even in khakis and a golfing sweater, he carried an air of military authority. She resisted the urge to fidget or salute.

Ginger Landis Renshaw stepped into the silence and extended her hand with a smile that seemed authentic. "Our apologies for showing up unannounced. We really should have called."

Her shoulder-length gray-blond hair was so perfectly styled, Gabrielle resisted the urge to smooth her hand over her own messy mop. She recalled from news reports that the woman was nearing sixty, but she carried the years well. Wearing a pale pink lightweight sweater set with pearls—and blue jeans—Ginger Landis wasn't at all what Gabrielle had expected. Thank goodness, because the woman in front of her appeared a lot less intimidating.

Gabrielle had seen her often enough on the news— always poised and intelligent, sometimes steely and determined. Today, a softer side showed as she looked at her stepson then over to Gabrielle.

"I'm Ginger. Nice to meet you, Gabrielle. Although I don't know exactly who I'm meeting since Hank isn't sharing anything beyond your name."

His eyes met hers. He really had left it to her to say what she wanted. She smiled her thanks.

"A pleasure to meet you, too, ma'am. Obviously, I'm a close friend of your stepson's." Taking the older woman's hand, Gabrielle smiled sheepishly and appreciated the light squeeze of encouragement. "He's been helping me with my son since my fiancé passed away."

There. Now she'd left it up to him to share what *he*

wanted with his family about who her fiancé was and what had happened overseas. She knew how Hank valued his privacy.

The collective sigh of relief that went through the four-some drew her attention back.

Ginger pressed a hand to her pearls. "So the baby isn't Hank's."

Oh, my God, they'd thought...?

Of course they had, and they must have been hurt by the thought that Hank would have had a child without telling them. He had to have known what they were thinking. Yet, he'd let them just hang there wondering while she got dressed? That took needing privacy to a whole new level.

Hank gestured to the younger couple. "This is my youngest stepbrother, Jonah. His wife, Eloisa. And their little girl named Ginger." He shot a look at Jonah. "Suck up."

Jonah pointed to his wife. "Her idea about naming our daughter after Mom. I'm putty in Eloisa's hands. Actually, I'm putty in her *and* our daughter's hands."

Hank rolled his eyes. "You'll remember Jonah since he's the one I spoke to about renting this house."

He shot his stepbrother a quick look, just short of an outright glare.

Jonah pointed to his wife again. "She pried it out of me." He hooked an arm around her waist. "I'm helpless when it comes to her. Remember?"

Ginger placed a hand on her stepson's arm. "We're sorry to burst in on you this way, but *Architectural Digest* is doing a photo shoot of this place to feature Jonah's restoration. It's a great boon for his business."

Hank mumbled to Jonah. "You didn't mention that, either."

"Didn't have time," Jonah said out of the corner of his

mouth. "Mom arranged it yesterday so she would have an excuse to come here. And besides, you weren't picking up your phone. That's what you get for ignoring your family."

The general chuckled softly.

Gabrielle was still stuck on the words *photo shoot.* "They'll be photographing the house?"

"And our family." Ginger smiled proudly. "Beyond being great publicity for Jonah's work, it's a lovely chance for me to show off my relatives without worrying about the paparazzi falling out of trees in the middle of a picnic just to get a picture for some cheap gossip rag."

Leonie better clean out her stash of reading material if she wanted to win Ginger's approval.

The general continued, "We've found if we periodically stage pictures on our own terms, the public gets bored enough to leave us alone for a while."

Ginger hooked an arm through Gabrielle's. "So, you'll join us for the photos? Friends are always welcome."

"I'm not sure what to say." The whole meeting was overwhelming.

"No need to make up your mind yet. I'm just glad to meet you." She squeezed Gabrielle's arm. "You'll have plenty of time to think it over while we unpack. Gentlemen, would you please unload the luggage from the car?"

Panic lit a bonfire in Gabrielle's stomach. She looked fast at Hank. Frustration mixed with resignation in his eyes.

His family was staying here.

"So you're okay with us staying here?" his father asked him.

Hank hefted suitcases from the back of the hybrid Mercedes SUV. "Yeah, General, sure."

"Son..."

His father had been a part of the Joint Chiefs of Staff, handling explosive world dynamics without breaking a sweat. But he still got cranky when his kids called him General. "Yeah, *Dad?*"

"That's better." The general nodded, walking alongside him, loaded down with luggage for such a short stay. Although half of it looked as if it belonged to Jonah and Eloisa's baby. A second car was parked behind Hank and Ginger's, a nondescript black sedan with two men in suits in the front—protective detail. His dad and Ginger kept at least one bodyguard at all times when away from home and undoubtedly extra security came from the royal side of the family.

No more making out on the lanai.

His father's strides matched his own. "Is the boy yours?"

Hank stopped short at the base of the steps. Was his dad calling him a liar? Wind rustled the hanging ferns and oak tree branches while he squelched his rising anger. "You heard Gabrielle say he isn't."

"Was she covering for you?" His father's eyes went into deep search mode, just as he'd done when single parenting his three teens.

Hank bit back the urge to just leave. It had chapped his hide, being questioned at sixteen, but it really burned now thinking his dad questioned his honor. "No one 'covers' for me, especially not Gabrielle. If Max was mine, you would have heard about it."

"You're not known for being chatty with the rest of the family," his father said dryly.

"Fair enough," he conceded. "But having a child is not something I would hide. Even if I decided to wait to tell you, I sure as hell wouldn't have let Gabrielle stand there alone, stating the kid is someone else's."

The doubt in his dad's eyes faded. "Of course. I should have known. You're an honorable man."

"Thanks for that much." He started up the back porch steps.

"You're also a private man, and that makes this a tough family for you to be a part of."

"Do ya' think?"

A laugh rumbled from his dad's barrel chest and yeah, it felt good to join in. The past week and a half had been beyond stressful. Good in a lot of ways—like hearing from the doctor that Max would be okay, and being with Gabrielle. But there was still enough baggage in their pasts to rival even the piles coming out of the back of that SUV.

His father stayed between him and the door. "So if the baby isn't yours, who's the dead fiancé she mentioned? I assume he'd be the father."

"My buddy Kevin, a pilot on my crew. He died in Afghanistan." Even those few words stoked the barely banked memories of his nightmare.

"Are you sure you know what you're doing here, son?"

He didn't need this kind of probing or interference. Not now. "Dad, I didn't ask for your opinion."

His old man's face creased with a smile. "That's never stopped me before. We don't get anywhere in the world if we sit around waiting to be asked."

"Okay, then. I won't *ask* if you mind if I leave." He turned away, ready to walk all the way around the house to another door, if need be.

"Her guy can't have been dead long." His father's words stopped him on the top step.

"Ten months," Hank answered without turning, the

smell of explosives and blood coming back so damn real he could have been over there, living that hell again.

Footsteps sounded on the wooden porch as his father neared. His large shadow stretched over Hank as it had done his entire life. "Son, are you sure she's through grieving? I'm not saying she's the wrong woman. I'm just saying be sure it's the right time."

The shadow shifted as the general backed away, leaving his words hanging out there to cast a shadow all their own. As much as Hank tried to live his own life, still his dad's legacy followed him. Was there something in the genetics that led him to make so many of the same choices his father had made, even when he worked his tail off to be different? Hell, his dad had even fallen for his friend's widow.

Did that mean a guy had to wait more than a decade to act on it?

Hank stayed standing on the top step long after his father gathered up the bags and headed inside.

While everyone else unpacked, Gabrielle sat with Ginger in the sunroom, little Ginger toddling around while Max napped in his baby swing. The moment felt so timeless, as if they could have been a family from a hundred years ago gathering just this way. If she were snapping photos for a magazine, Gabrielle would want these over any staged, fancy pictures.

She would want this life.

Well, other than the security detail walking the perimeter and talking into radios tucked in the cuff.

Her hands shaking, she gripped the arms of the rattan rocker. "Do you ever get tired of having bodyguards follow you everywhere?"

Ginger glanced out the wall of windows at the guards

as if she'd forgotten they were there. "Sure, but I try to remember it's just a part of the jobs I've been lucky enough to have." She swooped her granddaughter up into her arms and spun her around once. "Although being a grandmother is the best job on the planet."

"Better than being Secretary of State?"

"Hands down." Ginger set the giggling toddler on the floor and tugged Max's toe gently. "He's a sweet-natured baby. I hope you don't mind my asking...what are those little incisions on his stomach?"

How strange to have all that worry swept away in a few days. "He had surgery this week for a digestive disorder. He's fine now." She said another prayer of gratitude. "But that's why I'm here. At Hank's house, I mean. He's helping me out since this is his friend's baby. He's acting as a sort of a stand-in dad, I guess you could say."

Ginger sat on the rattan sofa next to her. "Although it's obvious Hank's your friend, too."

Was she asking out of curiosity or as a concerned relative? "We knew each other before..." Gabrielle picked at splinters on the armrest. "So yes, we're friends, too."

Ginger's hand fell on the Burberry diaper bag little Ginger's mother had left before she went upstairs to unpack. "I've known Hank since he was your son's age."

Really? "I thought you married the general more recently than that."

She was just realizing how little she knew about Hank beyond what she'd read in the papers. How much of that was even factual?

"My husband—my first husband—was in the air force with Hank, Sr." Her deep blue eyes, the same color as her son's, lit with nostalgia. "My husband Benjamin wasn't career military, like Hank. He wanted to serve for a few years, to give back to his country. Then he got out and went into politics."

Gabrielle recalled reading that Ginger had served the rest of her first husband's term after he'd died, then she turned out to be an even more savvy and effective politician than her husband. Her career had taken off from there. Even now, she served as an ambassador to a South American country. It was tough not to be intimidated by that much power and success. Gabrielle listened, wondering what the woman's agenda was in sharing her life story. Because no doubt, this savvy stateswoman would be every bit as tenacious in protecting her family as she was in negotiating for her country.

"While we were in the military—and I do mean we because the spouse sacrifices a lot being married to a service member—we were friends with Hank and Jessica. Our children played together, too. When Jessica died, I helped Hank with his children. He helped me with my boys after I lost Benjamin." She paused, staring out the sunroom windows and blinking back a shadowy grief that apparently even time hadn't dimmed. "There was never anything going on between us while either of our spouses were alive, nothing. Believe me, it shocked the hell out of both of us when our friendship turned into something more."

Gabrielle willed herself not to show the shame that dogged her still over that kiss she'd shared with Hank while Kevin was still alive. Kevin may have pardoned them with his dying breath, but she couldn't forgive herself.

She looked out over the lush Garden District lawn, seeking some of the answers or peace that Ginger also seemed to be looking for out the window. Instead, Gabrielle saw Hank. His long strides ate up ground as he made his way toward a bodyguard standing under a shady oak. Hands shoved in his pockets, he stopped alongside the security guy, just talking. Checking out the lay of the land, perhaps? Hank had put on a pin-striped button-down shirt with his jeans, rolled up sleeves and boat shoes. Yet he looked no less in command than he did in his uniform.

Like his father.

Ginger pressed her fingers to the corners of her eyes, drew in a bracing breath, then smiled again. "But we were talking about little Hank."

"*Little* Hank?"

"What can I say?" Ginger shrugged, smiling affectionately at her stepson on the lawn. "To me, he will always be that little boy racing his Big Wheel up and down the sidewalk. He loved to be outside, on the go. He led the pack even then. But he always played fair, too fair."

Gabrielle tore her eyes from Hank and put her focus back onto the conversation. She was reminded of her mother, the whole wonder woman, perfect mom and military wife persona that no human could hope to measure up to. "How can someone be too fair?"

Ginger leaned forward, elbows on her knees, her eyes steely blue with no holding back. She was apparently through taking the scenic route in their conversation. "He puts others before himself, sometimes to his own detriment."

"Are you saying I'm using him?"

"No, heavens no." She waved aside Gabrielle's guilty fears with a manicured hand. "I'm just saying he works so hard to be the good guy, he may not be telling you where he stands. Ask him what he wants. Don't assume. Ask, then ask again until he really talks."

Were there questions she should be asking Hank that she wasn't? Was it possible that Hank was only staying with her for the sake of being the good guy? He'd said it wasn't about a debt to Kevin anymore, but about wanting to be with her. Still. Even before Ginger said anything, Gabrielle had known that Hank was struggling with boundaries.

He'd really poured his heart out to her last night, leaving them both so emotionally raw that he'd needed some distance, seeking out Max rather than returning to bed with her. Obviously, he wasn't in the mood to share more, and quite frankly, she wasn't sure how much more either of them could take.

And Ginger thought she should dig even deeper?

Instead of helping her, Ginger's revelations only made her all the more afraid she wasn't the right person for Hank. She'd been taking, taking, taking from him since he'd stepped back into her life. He deserved someone who could give back, who could break through those high walls of his and care for him, as well. With each second that passed, the possibility of a future with Hank grew more complicated, more improbable.

Ginger shoved to her feet and swept the wrinkles from her jeans. "Enough serious talk for one day. Let's have some fun."

"Doing what?" Gabrielle grasped the subject change with both hands, eager to move on to safer ground.

"A local boutique is bringing clothes by for us to choose from for the photo shoot." Ginger clasped Gabrielle's hands in her own and tugged her to her feet. "Every new mom deserves an afternoon of spa pampering."

Eleven

Hank walked down the hall with a stealth picked up in military survival training. Although damned if he didn't feel about fifteen sneaking around so his dad wouldn't hear him slip into Gabrielle's room. He hadn't been able to steal even a few minutes alone with her since his family arrived. First his mother had abducted her all afternoon to try on dresses then supper had stretched out for hours as they alternated between subtly grilling Gabrielle and discussing the photo shoot for the next day.

Who knew his relatives had become such night owls?

This was his house, for God's sake. Well, his rental house for a short while longer. Not that it stopped anyone from claiming a spare room. Any minor sense of family boundaries had disappeared from his life long ago. He was seriously itching over the scrutiny, more so than usual.

His *father's* scrutiny dug even deeper than the prying

eye of a camera lens. What if his dad was right that Gabrielle wasn't over Kevin? What if she never got over loving and losing him?

Hank gripped the crystal doorknob outside her room. He'd hung out on the sidelines of her life once before and it had been pure hell. He didn't think he could do it again, not after having been with her. He'd claimed her, and he couldn't see letting her go again. The rest would have to work itself out.

He tapped once softly on Gabrielle's door before sliding inside. Her bed was empty, the covers still undisturbed.

Because she was slumped over her desk, asleep.

How often did she work herself into the ground this way? The afternoon spent trying on dresses with his stepmom must have cut into her schedule. He locked the doors to the hall and the nursery. Anyone wanting to find her would have to knock. His dad and stepmom were good people, but type-A sorts who tended to steamroll over people "for their own good."

Carefully, he slid his arms around her back and under her legs. Her hand slipped from the desk, her short nails sporting the light sheen of a pale pink polish. Ginger's doing, no doubt. His stepmom was a practical woman in many ways, but she did enjoy her manicures.

He scooped up Gabrielle against his chest, her satin robe parting to reveal a nightshirt. His mind zipped back to the uncomfortable interruption this morning in the library. She wasn't going to be caught half naked again.

Damn shame—as long as he was her only audience.

Gabrielle stirred in his arms. "Hank?"

"Shhh… Go back to sleep. I'm just moving you to the bed so you'll be more comfortable."

Her arm draped around his neck, her eyes groggy.

"Wait. Put me down. Almost done with the paper I have to turn in."

"Is it due tomorrow?" If so, he would be right there beside her, proofreading, if she needed him.

"Nuh-uh." Sleepy fog cleared from her eyes and they went smoky with awareness. She rested her other hand on his chest, her fingers tracing the vee of his collar. "Then you have time to finish it later."

"You're right. I do have time." She slipped a button free, then another. "For this."

She took his earlobe between her teeth and nipped.

A bolt of desire shot straight to his groin. He tightened his grip on her, pressing her closer. She smelled like lavender and Gabrielle, the scent so familiar now he could taste her on his tongue. He fought back the urge to take her right here.

He set her on the bed. More like, he dropped her and took a step back, trying his damnedest to be a gentleman. "You really should sleep."

"I've gotten plenty of sleep this past week, thanks to all the help from you and Leonie." She shrugged off her robe and whipped her nightshirt over her head, wispy blond hairs clinging to the cotton before it fell away. "Trust me to know what I *need*."

Call him a selfish bastard, but as he looked at her lounging on the bed wearing only a sea-green pair of bikini panties, he couldn't bring himself to tell her no.

"What *exactly* do you need?" He took off his watch and placed it on the bedside table with deliberate precision, setting his leather wallet alongside the lamp. He pulled a condom from his billfold, wanting her to know he would always protect her in every way possible. "Because I really want to hear every detail."

"You, here, doing whatever I say."

His eyebrows shot up. "Oh, really. You want—"

"Control. Do you have a problem with that?"

The challenge in her green eyes cranked him higher, his body more than happy to comply.

"None whatsoever." He tugged his shirt off, stepped out of his jeans and slipped into bed next to her. "What are you going to do with me now that you have me?"

Grabbing his shoulders, she shoved him onto his back, straddling him. "You'll have to wait and see."

"And how long will I have to wait?" He throbbed against the warm press of her satin underwear.

"Patience…" She wriggled just enough to tempt him without taking him over the edge. Biting back a groan, he squeezed his eyes shut, cupping her waist and guiding her faster against him.

She shifted to the side and he moved to catch her. Except she wasn't going anywhere. She tugged the sash from her robe and teased it along his chest in a slithering path. A playful smile spread over her face and she leaned forward to—

Holy crap, she was blindfolding him.

Wrapping the tie around and over his eyes twice, she sealed it in place with a kiss, pinning his wrists to the bed. And sure, he could have broken free and pulled it off at any time, but who was he to argue if she wanted control?

Willing his arms to relax, he sank back into the mattress, his head digging into the pillows and anchoring the blindfold. Her purr of approval stroked him with a heated sigh against his chest, soon replaced by her fingers. She used her touch, her lips, the glide of her hair along his skin in a feathery path that mirrored his game with the mask. She teased the silky strands along his shoulders over his chest until his skin tightened at the phantom touch.

Lower, lower still she trailed her hair until…the slide of the strands over his erection threatened to finish him before they'd even started. The lavender scent of her clung to the sash, filling him with each labored breath he dragged in.

Her hands replaced the feathery locks, stroking, caressing, driving him damn near crazy with wanting her. Then her mouth closed over him. His hands twisted in the sheets as he fought back the need to shout, she felt so damn good.

He reached to pull her up, and she shoved his arms away, continuing to take him higher with her lips, her tongue and then to hell with the blindfold. He ripped the sash from his face. "Okay, you win. If I don't get my hands on you soon, I'm going to lose my mind."

She pressed a kiss to his stomach, purring against his skin. "I'm all yours."

Thank God.

Hank hauled her up, flipping her to her back. He grabbed the condom from the bedside table, sheathing himself in record time before he thrust hilt deep inside her.

Holding her hands over her head, he drove into her again and again, watching her face to make sure she was every bit as crazed as he felt. Out of control? Totally. Something about this woman stole reasonable thought, tipping his whole world upside down.

She looked back up at him, her pupils wide and her chest flushing with pleasure, the signs he needed that she was close, too. Still, he held back, waiting, watching until…he saw her fly apart.

Only then did he allow himself to dive in with her, a hot release pumping from him, driving him into her again and again and even as he came, he already wanted more of her.

All of her. Gabrielle would be his wife and to hell with everything else.

And he intended to press hard and press now to make that happen before she slipped away.

Standing in front of the full-length mirror on the armoire door, Gabrielle struggled with the zipper on her new dress, scared of yanking too hard for fear she would damage the gown that cost more than she earned in a month. Who'd have thought a photo shoot of a "family dinner" would include a floor-length formal, complete with a manicure and an up-do? The nails and hair, she could live with and actually enjoyed.

But she'd been vaguely ill when she realized her clothing designer was the same one who'd once decked out Reese Witherspoon for the Oscars. Ginger had told her not to worry. They would be donating their dresses to a charity that raised funds for breast cancer survivors. Her conscience slightly assuaged, she'd accepted the "loaner" for the evening's photo shoot.

The plum-colored satin slid over her skin with reminders of all the ways she and Hank had used her robe's sash the night before. The power play of blindfolds and, later, bound hands had continued until nearly sunrise, leaving them both panting and depleted.

Their lovemaking also left her even more confused as to how they would blend their lives. She couldn't miss the seriousness in Hank's eyes, the intensity in his every move. Things were moving so fast. She wanted more time to figure things out before—if—they went public, but that option had ended the second his family walked into the foyer unannounced.

A tap sounded on the door. "It's me. Hank. Are you about ready?"

Pressing a palm to her chest, she held the dress in place, while hitching up the hem with her other hand and padding barefoot to let him in. She unlocked the door and started to tell him she'd changed her mind about being in the photo shoot, such a public declaration of their relationship no matter what his stepmother said.

She darn near swallowed her tongue. Hank in his formal air force uniform filled the doorway and her eyes. Rows of medals gleamed on his chest, his silver aviator wings pinned above them. She'd seen him dressed this way before, but she'd always been with Kevin, so she'd worked to keep her distance, putting those walls in place between them.

Right now, Hank was one-hundred-percent touchable. Her hand fell to rest right over his heart. "You take my breath away."

"I should be saying that to you," he said, without even looking at her dress. His eyes stayed firmly on her face.

She touched his tie, his chin, his mouth that had brought her so much pleasure the night before. If only they could lock themselves in her room. But they couldn't. There were people waiting downstairs and a photo shoot to complete.

Which reminded her— "I need your help zipping my dress, please."

"As long as I get to unzip it later." He backed her into the bedroom, kicking the door closed behind him. He set something on top of the armoire, then turned her around. He kissed her neck before she could look at what he'd brought in with him. His lips lingered as he inched the zipper up. Her head fell back until he grazed his mouth over hers.

Easing away, she said, "I'm not sure I should be in the pictures. What if people assume…more than they should?"

"They'll assume you're my date, which you are. They may even assume we're lovers, which is true, as well." His hands tracked the dip of her waist, the curve of her hips. "Or they'll assume the photos have been staged with a drop-dead sexy model on my arm."

He palmed her stomach and pulled her flush against his thickening arousal.

"Hank, are you sure we can't just ditch the whole thing? Leonie already has Max for the night. We could lock ourselves in here or walk by Lake Ponchartrain holding hands."

"Either option sounds infinitely more exciting than this dinner. If you're serious about wanting to ditch the gathering, then that's what we'll do."

She was tempted to do just that, but Ginger's words filtered through, reminding her how he always put other people's needs first. "Your family will be upset with you, and I don't want to cause trouble."

"Their opinion has never stopped me before."

Except if he cut out on his stepmother's plans—plans Ginger had concocted just to be a part of his life—there would be deep disappointment. No matter how many boundaries he put in place, Hank clearly loved his relatives, even if he preferred a little less togetherness than the others did.

She rested her arms over his as he hugged her from behind. Smiling at him in the mirror, she willed her nervous doubts away. "Let's go to dinner, and then we can take that walk along the lake."

"If you're sure."

"I am." Sort of.

"Okay, then. We have a date for later. As for now…"
He leaned past her to pull a flat velvet jewelers box off
the top of the armoire.

He creaked open the lid, revealing a wide bracelet band
of diamonds with matching chandelier earrings.

She gasped, in awe of the beauty and in horror at what
the price tag must have been. "Hank, I can't—"

"Wear them for the photos," he interrupted. He clasped
the bracelet around her wrist and passed her the earrings
with enough diamonds to make the down payment on
a house. "If you have any arguments, take it up with
Ginger."

Even as he said it, she knew he was the one behind the
jewels. She put on one earring, then the other. "And if I
lose one of these in the soup?"

He grabbed her shoulders and turned her to face him,
tiered diamonds brushing her neck. "Gabrielle, they're
just earrings."

"Diamond earrings." Lots of diamonds.

"I've never given a damn about money before, but I
find myself wanting to spend it on you, to make your life
easier."

She stroked his rugged face, his intensity tugging at
her far more than any jewels. "Thank you, but I'm not
exactly the kept-woman type."

"It could be more than that." He pulled her hand from
his face and held on. "You could move in with me. Most
of your classes are online now anyway. I can help you
with Max."

Her chest tightened with increasing panic.

"Hank, stop. I've worked hard for this life I've built
here in New Orleans. Let's not rush into anything."

"Rush? I've been halfway in love with you for nearly
two years. Doesn't feel like rushing to me. We were

friends before. We're lovers now." His voice grew tighter and tenser with each angry word. "Damn it, if I had my way, we'd just get married."

Her throat closed up. He'd shocked her silent, *scared* her silent. The roots of her hair tingled, and she struggled for air. She wanted to be with him, was probably halfway in love with him, as well.

His backhanded proposal touched her, without question, tempted her even. But the thought of getting married? No matter what he said about how long they'd known each other, taking such a huge step was definitely too much, too soon for her to handle.

Hank's jaw flexed, his eyes chilling. "Your enthusiasm is overwhelming."

Oh, God, she'd hurt him. She clasped his hand. "Hank, you just surprised me. I don't know what to say."

He let go, shoulders broad and braced in his uniform. "Let me make this easy so you don't have to work on concocting excuses. My dad thinks I should give you more time to get over Kevin. Do you still love him?"

"It's not that simple."

His face closed up. "It is to me."

How had this conversation gotten so out of control? How had her *life* gotten so out of control? She struggled for the right words to defuse the situation. "Kevin and I were having problems. You know he and I argued before the deployment about my leaving New Orleans and moving closer to him. And now you're pushing me to make the same decision."

"Is that what you and Kevin really fought about right before we deployed?" He pinned her with too perceptive eyes.

She looked away. "Of course it is."

"But the two of you had been debating that for months.

I don't know why I didn't see it at the time, but something different must have happened that day, something bigger."

His perception made her itchy. She wanted to leave the past behind her, but that would never be possible with Hank. Their lives were too entwined. "We'd been fighting because the one time I got tipsy, we forgot to use a condom, okay? Are you happy now?" She jammed her feet into the silver heels. "Let's go to dinner."

Hands behind his back, feet planted, he blocked the door. "I'm not happy but I want to hear it all."

What was he hoping to accomplish by pushing this now? Why couldn't he just take his father's advice on this and give her some time?

She did care for Hank, so much, and the thought of losing him scared her almost as much as the thought of moving forward too quickly. She needed to make him understand what had happened between her and Kevin, to share things she'd held back before.

"That day, we fought about it again because he wanted me to go some party with him and I didn't want to go drinking. I wanted to just be together before he left. Maybe I was looking for some reassurance because things were already rocky between us."

Hank's stoic face didn't give her any indication of whether or not she was getting through to him. She'd been so focused on helping him through his grief over seeing Kevin die, she hadn't considered for an instant that he might be jealous. But she couldn't ignore the possibility now. "Before I could even see it coming we were fighting. I was tired of always having to be the responsible one. Always having to be the grown-up...like with partying and birth control."

The next part was tougher, her words coming back to

haunt her and hurt her. "I told him I wasn't ready for a family. I didn't want to be my mom."

And to think her precious baby boy had already been growing inside her. She'd been working so hard to make it up to Max for not wanting him at the start.

Her voice dipped lower. "I didn't tell Kevin about being pregnant because I was afraid he would throw that fight back in my face."

Hank scrubbed his jaw as if he didn't know what to think. "Why didn't you tell me all of this before?"

"Excuse me for not wanting to talk to you about details from mine and Kevin's sex life."

She'd never shared the truth with anyone. The fight had been private, between her and her fiancé, and no matter what had happened with Hank back then, Kevin had deserved that kind of loyalty.

"I mean, why didn't you tell me the two of you were having problems, deeper than just whether or not to move?" Anguish and anger mixed in his eyes. "Do you know how much I've beaten myself up over kissing you that night?"

"I beat myself up, too. But, back then, I didn't want to betray Kevin's trust by sharing something so personal. And now, I guess I thought it didn't matter."

"There were two of us kissing, and even if we didn't have a relationship then, I thought we were still friends. So yeah, it mattered."

Would things have been different if she'd been more open with Hank that day? She wasn't sure how she could have been so honest with him when she hadn't even been able to be honest with herself. Since nothing else seemed to be working, she tried to shift the tone of the conversation back to lighter ground. "Do you think we could just go back to me tying you to the bedpost?"

His shoulders tensed.

"Not funny. Not now," he snapped, his anger not fooling her for a second.

She saw the depth of his pain, and she didn't have a clue how to make things better. Damn it, she hurt, too. Why was he doing this now? Why was he pushing her for something so soon? "Tell me what you want me to do."

"You don't have to *do* anything. It's not about you being in control in bed or in the relationship I thought we were starting." He shook his head, stuffing his fists in his uniform pockets. "You keep talking about not wanting to be your mother, but you're pulling the same control act that she does. You're driving yourself into the ground trying to prove you don't need anyone."

"That's not fair." She'd come to the house with him. Allowed others to care for her son. To care for her. She was giving up control left and right.

"But it's honest."

His clipped words iced over her. A warning prickled along her skin.

"If you can't accept me as I am, there's no way this will work." She'd fought too long and hard to carve out her independence to throw it away as soon as Hank Renshaw looked her way. She wanted him desperately. That didn't mean she would give up control of her life with both hands.

The silence stretched.

The space between them might as well have been miles. And then she knew: there was no reaching him. His father had even tried—and astutely so. Hank talked about her being a control freak and yet he was trying to call all the shots.

She waited for him to tell her she was wrong, to tell her all the ways this would be fine. But just as Kevin had balked when she didn't live up to his expectations of perfection, Hank was bailing on her, and the failure hurt even more this time.

What a helluva time to realize there was no halfway measure to her feelings. She'd fallen totally and completely in love with Hank Renshaw.

Twelve

Since Hank first saw Gabrielle, he'd wondered what would have happened if he'd met her before Kevin did. What if he'd had the chance to win her over?

Now he'd been given that chance, and he'd blown it in less than two weeks.

Gabrielle's cool hand was tucked in the crook of his arm as he walked down the stairs for the photo shoot. His father waited in the foyer alongside Ginger. His dad wore the same uniform as Hank did, but with stars on his shoulder boards and a chest so full of medals it was a wonder the old man could still stand upright. His wife—Ginger—stood beside him all decked out in red and smiles. She'd maneuvered this whole gathering with such expectations. Had his family's arrival made things worse or simply exposed the inevitable?

Hell if he knew that or anything else right now.

His whole world was exploding out of control and there

wasn't a damn thing he could do about it. Just like when his mother had died, when his sister had been kidnapped, when Kevin had died, nothing he did changed the outcome.

From the foyer, the cameraman clicked, clicked, clicked pictures, snapping shots as fast as rapid gunfire, taking Hank back to that battlefield moment when he'd lost Kevin. Flashes blinded him until he fought the urge to duck. His mouth dried up. He couldn't force Gabrielle to accept what he had to offer. He could only keep putting one foot in front of the other as he had his whole life.

At any other time, Gabrielle would have enjoyed the staged dinner, with all its pageantry of the local history. But right now, it took everything inside her to hold it together through this family event. She couldn't even enjoy the magnificent dress and jewelry. But she refused to embarrass Hank by running crying from the house. She would see this dinner through, then decide where to go next with her son.

Forcing back the urge to flee, she blinked away tears and plastered on a smile as strains of Beethoven piped through the home's sound system. The dining room had been transformed into everything she would have wished for if the house had been hers. Greenery had been scattered throughout to fill in the sparser corners. The sideboard was laden with silver chafing dishes and serving pieces, a server standing discreetly to the side.

A candelabrum spiraled up from the table with a spray of roses and stephanotis trailing down the middle. Crystal, china and silver place settings were set for—she counted—sixteen.

Sixteen?

She glanced over quickly at Ginger and the general,

then at Jonah in his tuxedo with his wife in a glittering gold gown. Who else was slated to arrive and why had Ginger not mentioned it before?

The doorbell rang and the floodgates opened.

Gabrielle took a step back instinctively as all of the Renshaw and Landis offspring poured into the foyer. Ginger's other three sons arrived with their wives, and the general's two daughters trailed behind with their husbands. The whole group filled the space in a mix of more uniforms, designer gowns and a mint's worth of jewels. Introductions passed in a blur of names and photos before they began to take their seats at the monster-size table. Hank held out her chair for her, a silent looming presence behind her. His hand brushed her back briefly before stepping away.

And if this event had been orchestrated for Ginger to meet Gabrielle, then they'd all been called here, as well, to inspect her. No wonder Hank had such rigid boundaries.

She glanced up at him just as his stepbrother leaned toward him while keeping his arm draped around wife.

"Did they forget to tell you the whole family was invited to the photo shoot? They're all staying in another house they rented two streets over."

"*You* neglected to tell me," Hank growled under his breath while his stepmother raved over one of the women's gowns. "Don't bother recycling that excuse about being putty in your wife's hands. If I'd known, I wouldn't be here subjecting myself to this zoo."

"And you wonder why no one tells you anything." Jonah's wife laughed softly beside him. "In this case, however, I can honestly say I thought you already knew. Maybe Ginger thought the general told you and vice versa."

"You don't believe that any more than I do. This was a setup, clean and simple."

Gabrielle gripped his arm tighter. "For what purpose?"

His guarded eyes met hers. "So you could see what you're letting yourself in for, getting involved with this family."

"That seems a little extreme." She eyed the length of the table, her ears burning with the sense that everyone was talking about her.

Jonah shrugged. "Extreme? Maybe. But I've learned to go with the flow."

Easier said than done with their fight hanging over her head. But Gabrielle went through the motions all the same, answering questions from the mass of family by rote. They were wonderful people who at any other time she would have enjoyed. But allowing herself to form an attachment to any of them would only set her up for more heartache.

She hardly tasted the tapas or rich cabernet that was served with them. All through the five-course dinner, she could only think of Hank. His proposal. And how differently that offer could have played out six months from now when they'd both gained more distance from the deployment, her son's health scare and Kevin's death.

By dessert, she was ready to shatter from holding her feelings in check for fear the photographer would capture a shot of her heart in her eyes as she stared at Hank. So she kept right on smiling at stories about all the cute nieces and nephews until the candles burned low.

The doorbell pierced the mingled sounds of classical music, clanking dishes and laughter. One of the three wait staff peeled away from the sideboard and into the hall to answer the door. Ginger's face creased with worry, although no one would have gotten by the security outdoors without decent identification.

Soft voices from the hall carried into the dining room.

Familiar voices.

Gabrielle gaped in disbelief at Ginger. "You invited my parents, too?"

Ginger's eyes went wide with surprise. "Your parents?" Then her features smoothed, and she sent a pointed glance toward the photographer as she stood. "What a pleasant surprise."

Jonah brought his napkin to his lips and said out of the corner of his mouth. "We're gonna need a bigger house."

"Gabrielle?" Her mother's voice grew louder, closer, her German accent light after so many years of living around the world. "Where's the baby? Where's my grandson?"

Chairs scraped back. The general pivoted toward the cameraman, his looming frame and military command blocking the photographer. Her parents stood in the archway between the foyer and dining room—her mother looking travel-worn from the transcontinental journey. They weren't dressed with the glitz of Hank's family, but her parents had worked hard to build a life for their kids, even if those hopes sometimes pushed her mother into micro-managing their lives.

Ginger swept up beside them. "Sergeant and Mrs. Ballard—Christine and Edward—" of course Hank's well-briefed, savvy stepmom already knew her parents' names "—welcome!"

Gabrielle skirted around the table and to her parents, ever aware of silent, brooding Hank only a step behind her. Not that she would have expected otherwise. Hank might be angry at her, frustrated with her, even irreconcilably so, but he would always do the honorable thing. He wouldn't embarrass her in front of his family or hers.

She hugged her burly dad, then her mother. The familiarity of her mom's arms and familiar gardenia cologne comforted her in spite of all the tension and heartache threatening to floor her.

She took her mother's hands and whispered. "Mom, what are you and Dad doing here?"

"I'm so sorry to have disrupted your big event." Her mother eyed her gown and jewels with a hint of disapproval. "I didn't know there would be so many people...."

Hank thrust his hand out. "Mrs. Ballard, Sergeant Ballard, I'm Hank Renshaw. It's a pleasure to have you here. Let's go across to the library and talk for a moment while the staff sets a place for you both."

And while Hank's stepmom likely booted out the photographer.

Jonah's wife reached out to Gabrielle, as the other wives clustered in a semicircle, creating a wall of privacy between her and the prying lens. The family moved in seamless sync, having made a science out of handling the media.

Hank ushered her parents across the hall into the library to give them privacy, and Gabrielle couldn't help but think how only yesterday morning she'd come in here to find him asleep with her son on his chest. The world was moving at warp speed.

The doors closed, sealing them in the cavernous room that hadn't been staged for the photo shoot. Empty shelves climbed to the ceiling, as hollow as her heart.

Her mother's face relaxed, and she grabbed her daughter's hands. "We're here to check on you and help. Although it appears you have plenty of helping hands." Her eyes zipped back and forth from her to Hank, curiosity crackling, even as she continued to ramble, "You said you just had Hank's help, and I know it's not P.C. to say so, but a man's help with a baby isn't the same as a woman's help."

An image popped to mind of Hank asleep with Max on his chest, and she almost burst into tears, which would be absolutely *the* worst thing to do around her parents now. Yet, something inside her felt about five years old, and she wanted nothing more than to pour out her heart to her mom while drinking a cup of hot cocoa.

What in the world was Hank saying to her father over in the corner?

Her mother wrapped her arm around her shoulders. "We're staying at a lovely little bed-and-breakfast just down the road. We would have come earlier, but we had to wait for the Mardi Gras travelers to leave town. We're comfortable there with plenty of room. We got a suite, in case you needed somewhere to stay while your apartment's being fixed. We weren't sure exactly what you had set up here with your gentleman friend."

Because Gabrielle hadn't told her. She'd closed herself off from her parents, more intensely than before over these past ten months for fear they would judge her life, her decision to have a child alone.

For fear she would become a child again around them and just let her mother take control.

But she couldn't stay here after the fight with Hank.

These were her parents. Her heart was breaking, and yes, she needed a soft place to land tonight. She wasn't running away from Hank. She just wanted room to clear her head, something she couldn't do with an audience of nearly twenty relatives.

Besides, she owed her parents that much. They'd flown

all this way to see her baby, her dear son that had an-
chored her in spite of all the hurt clawing at her heart.

"Mom," she blurted out, the last thing she would have
expected to ever come out of her mouth. "Max and I
would love to spend some time with you and Dad. Give
me ten minutes to change and toss some things in a suitcase."

"Don't you think it's a little early in the day for alcohol?"

Parked on the lanai, Hank ignored his father and tipped
back the imported beer. His dad did always have the good
stuff on hand. As he sat here, looking out at the yard, tormenting the hell out of himself with memories of dancing with Gabrielle under the stars, he couldn't think of a
better time to get falling-down drunk.

She'd just up and left with her parents last night, gathered her son and headed out the door, only pausing long
enough to hug his mother. Holding Max for all of ten
seconds to say goodbye had damn near torn his already
bruised heart from his chest. He'd thought he heard Gabrielle murmur a tearful thanks before she booked it out
of his life. But what the hell was he supposed to do?

The morning sure hadn't brought any answers so by
noon he'd moved his moody self outside away from his
hovering family.

He looked up at his father. "Want a beer anyway?"

"Sure." His dad dropped into a chair beside him, and
pulled a bottle from the crystal ice bucket Hank had
brought outside. "But only so you aren't drinking alone."

"Damn nice of you."

"Count yourself lucky. I'm the only one of the family
willing to put up with your bad mood."

Hank set his bottle down with controlled precision,

anger pumping through him. "With all due respect, sir, I didn't ask you to come here. I didn't ask for your help, which sucked by the way."

His father cocked his head to the side. "How so?"

"You're the one who said she needed time to grieve for her dead fiancé. I don't think the Landis-Renshaw clan gave her much time by sweeping in here unannounced. Do you?"

"So you love her?"

Hank reached for the bottle and clammed up again.

The general reclined in the chair, eyes too astute. "That had to have made things tough for you, having feelings for Gabrielle while they were dating."

"What makes you think I had feelings for her back then?" he asked evasively.

"You haven't even been home from your deployment for two weeks and you're not the type to fall for someone fast."

"You would be wrong about that." He'd fallen for Gabrielle the first time her saw her.

His father lifted and eyebrow and his beer. "Oh, really?"

"Wow, I stepped right into that, didn't I?"

"It helps that I know you."

Hell, might as well quit pretending. He sank back into his chair. A strange—and uncomfortable—suspicion drifted through his head. "Did you have feelings for Ginger when Mom was alive?"

"Ginger and I were both married, both in love with our spouses. Then we were both busy as hell bringing up kids." His face creased with...pain? "I can honestly say the feelings came to us later. We wasted a lot of years avoiding it. Tough for a guy like me to admit he was afraid, but I was a big coward. Scared of losing a woman I loved again."

He looked at his big, invincible three-star father through different eyes. "What helped Ginger get over the fear?"

And could that be helpful to Gabrielle?

"You would have to ask Ginger yourself."

"Really?" He shook his head. "Sorry, Dad, but that sounds like a damn awkward conversation."

Ginger had been a part of his life for as long as he could remember, but he didn't exactly excel at the warm, fuzzy parts of family relationships.

"Believe it or not, she's handled tougher cases than you. She's a damn fine diplomat."

"Things just aren't that simple for me. Talk it over and make it all better."

"It can be."

"What about Kevin?" His fingers tightened on the longneck. He met his dad's eyes and let the hurt just roll right over him, regardless of whether or not his father read it in his eyes. "I just say to hell with the fact I made a move on her before he died?"

"That must have been a real bite in those honorable intentions of yours," his father stated simply, not judging, just putting the undeniable fact out there.

"Tough to reconcile." Until he did, he couldn't see a way through to being with Gabrielle although he'd thought more than once that he wanted to be a husband to her and a father to Max. He still wanted those things, but he'd certainly botched his proposal. He understood now that he had to reconcile that guilt first or he would continue to sabotage their relationship again and again.

Kevin could pardon him a hundred times over but until Hank could forgive himself, there was no way to move forward. He could see now that the fight with Gabrielle wasn't about where she would live or which one of them was in control. Because Kevin was steering their relationship, even from the grave.

"Son, it's time to stop punishing yourself for being alive when he isn't."

"Easier said than done." He bit back the urge to shout, anger piling on top of frustration. "You're going to have to excuse me for being slow on the uptake, but this conversation is supposed to help me how? Because the way I see it, I'm sitting here, with my gut on fire and no way out."

"Your gut's on fire? Good." Hank clapped him on the shoulder. "Then you're almost there...."

"You're glad I'm about to put my fist through a wall?"

The general didn't so much as wince, just looked back with wise eyes and a face that was beginning to show the toll of numerous wars. "We spend a lot of time pumping ourselves up for battle. You have to believe you're invincible to hang tough during some of the things we're called to do in the line of duty. That's a difficult switch to turn off once we come home."

Damn straight, he was wired tight. And come to think of it, he had made going after Gabrielle into a personal mission.

He focused on his father's words, looking for something to grab hold of before the grief and rage pulled him under. "Makes sense."

"Screw what makes sense," his dad barked. "Quit thinking logically. Quit running scared. It hurt like hell to lose your best friend, all the worse to be there when it happened. There's only one way to get to the other side of that grief so you can claim the good that's waiting for you."

Each breath seared his throat. "And what would that be?"

"Wade right in."

His dad's words—his dad's wisdom—sliced through the last of his reserves. Hank squeezed his eyes closed as a tear rolled down his cheek. His father's hand fell to rest on his shoulder and finally, Hank let himself grieve.

Thirteen

The quiet was deafening today as opposed to the evening before with Hank's family.

Gabrielle curled up in the quaint little brass daybed in the bed-and-breakfast suite her parents had booked yesterday. Max was asleep. Her parents had gone out for a walk before supper. Surprisingly, her mom hadn't pushed for details.

Leaving Hank's house yesterday had been a crazy whirlwind of throwing things in her bag and gathering her son. Leonie had been confused but busy taking care of Hank's nieces and nephews. Gabrielle had just wanted to get out before she burst into tears, a close call when Hank had held Max to say goodbye.

Once at the bed-and-breakfast, she had slept and slept, and part of her knew she was grieving over losing Hank but she couldn't find a way out from under the confusion and hurt of her argument with him. The longer she was away from him, the more difficult it seemed to find her way through to reconciliation.

The outside door clicked with the opening lock a second before her parents walked through. Her burly daddy, who rarely said much, lumbered into her room with a small white box in his hands. He set the confection store carton on the end table and dropped a quick kiss on top of her head.

"Love you, Gabby girl."

Then he was gone. Much like her growing up years. She'd always been sure of his love but his presence had been in short supply. He passed her mother coming in as he ducked out to his room. The television vibrated lightly through the wall, the sports channel no doubt.

Her mother still hovered across the room. "Do you mind if I sit and join you? Those pralines your dad bought are to die for."

"Sure, Mom, knock yourself out." She nudged the box toward her mother.

Dropping into a fat floral chair by the window, Christine pulled one of the caramel pecan treats from the box, breaking off a bite at a time as she nibbled and stared out the window. Gabrielle kept waiting for the lecture or third degree, but it never came.

Finally, she couldn't stand the pressure of waiting any longer. "Go ahead and ask, Mom."

Her mother looked over quizzically, smoothing back her short blond bob. "Ask what?"

"About Hank and me. You came all this way, so you might as well say your piece."

"I came all this way because my grandson had surgery and this was the soonest I could leave your little sisters. And I came to meet this new man in your life who's obviously very important to you."

"He's not in my life anymore." Gabrielle eyed the box of pralines, but her stomach hurt so badly she couldn't eat.

"Looked to me last night like you're a major part of his life and family." Her mother popped another bite in her mouth.

Gabrielle hugged her knees. "That party was all for show, staged for a magazine shoot."

"I'm not talking about the fancy dinner. I'm talking about the expression in his eyes when he looks at you. That man loves you."

Just hearing those words cut right through her heart. "Mom, he may have had feelings for me, but we never stood a chance. Anything we had would have always been tangled up in his survivor's guilt. He will always see me as his best friend's girl and that's not something I can fight."

"Do you still see yourself as Kevin's fiancée?"

That stopped her short. "Of course not. I understand that Kevin is gone, and I'm helpless to change that."

"*Helpless?* That's a strange word choice. Why would you feel helpless?"

Gabrielle gawked at her mother. "You've got to be kidding. How could I feel anything but helpless?"

Her mother set aside the praline, her attention zeroing in. "There's nothing you could have done for Kevin. You're not Wonder Woman."

A dark snort of laughter burst from her. "That's rich, coming from you. You're the ultimate wonder woman. You make everything look easy."

"Now that's just silly, dear. Life is anything but easy." Her mother moved smoothly from the chair to sit beside Gabrielle on the bed. "Being a military wife and mother is full of tough challenges."

She searched her mom's face for some sense that her mom was joking but found only complete honesty. Her mother truly didn't see herself as the conquer-all woman everyone else perceived her to be. "Why didn't you ask for help?"

"What was complaining going to get me? My family was an ocean away. My husband was getting shot at in another country. And I had five children to take care of." She flattened her hands to her thighs. "Honest to God, I didn't have time to complain."

Gabrielle understood that feeling well enough lately.

"If there had been help available, I would have embraced it with both hands. For more time to read to my kids. Or even to read a book for myself while soaking in a bubble bath." She sighed, rolling her green eyes in imaginary bliss.

Gabrielle's heart ached as she thought of how perceptive Hank had been about her wish for a long soak alone, saturating herself in lavender-scented bubbles. Some might consider that a small thing, but seeing her mother brought a hefty reminder of Ballard family values— thoughtfulness, doing things for others, that's what mattered more than money.

Christine took her daughter's hands in hers. "It's not like I knew how to handle everything in those days. You just don't remember the burned meals or the time I wrecked the car because I forgot to pick your brother up at kindergarten, then I drove too fast scared to death because I was late. Believe me, I cried then. As for the Wonder Woman issue…" Her mother's German accent got stronger when she was fired up, turning her *W*s into *V* sounds. "I am not perfect now, just better at handling things than I was then."

Could her mother be right? That she'd simply forgotten

the more frazzled days? "If you learned over time, don't I deserve the same chance?"

"You have a point." She stroked back Gabrielle's hair as she'd done millions of times, always there, always loving, and that did count for a lot. "I know I interfere quite often. What is it they call that here in the States... Being an airplane mother?"

Gabrielle grinned. "A helicopter mom, always hovering."

"Ah, that makes more sense. I never understood the airplane analogy."

Smiling, Gabrielle leaned into her mom and they laughed together.

Her mother's arm slid around her shoulders. "Do you love this man? Do you love Hank?"

Gabrielle didn't even have to think to know. The truth settled in her heart, the only thing that made sense in her life. Why was it, though, that love had to always bring so much pain? "Yes, Mom, I love Hank more than I've loved anyone in my life, except for my son."

For once, she didn't feel guilty about admitting she did have deeper feelings for Hank than she'd had for Kevin. She had loved Kevin and she'd done her best to be a good fiancée, staying with the relationship longer than she should have. If anything, she'd hurt him most by hanging on too long when there'd been signs the relationship might not be a good fit.

Her mother hugged her tighter. "Then you don't need to have all the perfect answers right now. No one is a wonder woman from day one. Do the best you can, don't give up and the rest will sort itself out with time if you are determined to work at it."

Her mother's advice shuffled around inside her until it settled, making such perfect sense she didn't know why she hadn't seen it before. She didn't have to have every-thing figured out before moving forward. It was okay to love Hank and be with Hank while they resolved their problems, because yes, she *did* want to find a way to be with the man she loved. Forever. "I am determined, Mom. Very much so."

"Then what are you sitting around here for? Go get your man. Your father and I welcome the chance to baby-sit our grandson."

Complete love and acceptance radiated from her mother's face. Unconditional love, just like she felt for Max. Gabrielle wrapped her arms around her mom and held on tight.

"Danke, Mama." She adored the nuances of her mother's language. *Danke.* Thank you, but less formal for a family member. A loved one. *"Danke."*

And now she just hoped she wasn't too late to claim Hank's love that she'd so foolishly almost tossed away.

Family dinners two nights in a row?

Hank felt as if he'd set a new record in togetherness. But his relatives had all come to New Orleans for *him*. He couldn't just boot them out of town. So he parked himself at the table while everyone spoke on top of each other. They weren't there to intrude. They simply wanted to be a part of his life, see him after his deployment and show him some love.

And after his conversation with his father earlier, he had to confess that the whole Renshaw-Landis connection was starting to grow on him. He would have to be thick-headed not to recognize the gift of this much support—a room full of people who would drop everything for him.

Tonight's meal was less formal than the photo shoot dinner. Instead of gowns, uniforms and tuxedos, everyone wore jeans or khakis. The children were included, too, the table packed with high chairs and chatter about elementary school plays. The menu ranged from Creole shrimp and grits to hot dogs with macaroni and cheese. Still, even with nearly thirty kids and adults seated, the table seemed lacking to him without Gabrielle and Max.

Since that talk with his father, he'd been wracking his brain on how to win her back in a way that still gave her the time and space she needed. He refused to accept failure. He needed to be smart about this. His whole future was at stake.

As he speared another fat Gulf shrimp that was totally wasted on him tonight, the doorbell rang and Leonie raced to answer it.

Frowning, he set his fork back on the plate. The general raised an eyebrow and two of his stepbrothers shot to their feet.

What the hell? While he knew no one would get by security without the proper identification, it would be helpful if they started announcing some of these unexpected guests. What family members were left?

"Hank?"

His ears had to be fooling him, creating the sound of the voice he wanted to hear more than anything.

Then miraculously, so damn amazingly, Gabrielle stood in the archway to the dining room. His heart got stuck somewhere in his throat. He pushed his chair back and stood, ignoring the weight of his family's eyes all trained on him. He could see only Gabrielle, with her wind-flushed cheeks and her loose, silky blond hair.

Most of all, he saw her beautiful smile.

Relief scoured through him. For whatever reason, she'd come back to him, and he would be damned before he did or said one thing to push her away again. So he smiled back at her, but waited, letting her take the lead for now.

Gabrielle walked deeper into the dining room, her sexy legs striding confidently closer. "I'm sorry to disturb everyone's dinner. Would you mind if I stole Hank from you? I'm not sure I'll bring him back anytime soon. In fact, I may want to keep him for a very, very long time."

Laughter rippled down the table, and he didn't miss how one of his sisters shouted that Gabrielle was welcome to hang on to him permanently.

His stepmother reached for Gabrielle's hand. "I'm so glad you came back."

Gabrielle smiled full out, not a shadow in sight. "Me, too."

Past ready to have her to himself, Hank palmed her waist and followed her out into the foyer before facing her. At first, there were no words. He just took in the beauty of her face that he'd dreamed of so often while he was overseas. The thought of not having her in his life…

He swallowed down a lump in his throat and cupped her shoulders, needing to touch her. "What brought you here tonight?"

Her hands fell to rest on his chest. "I have a surprise for you."

"Your arrival is plenty of a surprise."

"Not by a long shot. Now close your eyes." A mischievous glint lit her emerald eyes. "Trust me."

And he did. He trusted her with his love and his life.

Hank shut his eyes, hopeful as hell that this was going to go well for him. A silky cloth trailed over his fingers, up his arm then over his eyes. Realization slid over him just as Gabrielle tied the blindfold behind his head.

Oh, yeah.

Hank clasped her wrist, his thumb stroking her racing

pulse. "I assume I'll be keeping my clothes on for now since my family's in the next room."

"You're every bit as safe in my hands as I am in yours." Her voice caressed his senses, the words as satiny as the fabric she'd teased over his skin.

Hooking her arm with his, she guided him smoothly toward the back of the house and out the door. The cool evening air wrapped around him while he waited for her next move.

Gabrielle rested her head against his shoulder. "My car's a tighter fit than yours so you'll need to watch your head stepping inside."

So they were leaving. Interesting. But anything Gabrielle did intrigued him, always had. "We can take mine if you prefer. The keys are in my pocket."

"Hmm.... Sounds like you're propositioning me." The tips of her fingers hooked in the front pocket of his jeans.

"I'm hopeful, Gabrielle, but taking nothing for granted."

He could have sworn he felt her lips brush his shoulder, but then his mind focused completely on her hand dipping in to fish out his keys with what had to be deliberate precision. She pulled back out slowly, her fingers rubbing against his increasing arousal.

A low growl rumbled in his throat. "I really hope we're alone out here."

"The security guard has his back to us. He's watching the street."

"I can't wait to get inside the car with you—only you."

"Patience, Hank. I promise this will all be worth it."

With that vow hanging between them, she led him smoothly to his SUV and settled them both inside. Seconds later, they were on the road, with her behind the wheel and him still blindfolded. While he was a navigator, even he started to lose any sense of direction after a few minutes of her speeding around curves and turns.

He resisted the urge to grab for the armrest. "You drive like a maniac."

"I learned on the autobahn." The car veered left hard and fast before jerking to a halt.

"How did I not know this about you before?"

"We have a lot to learn about each other, and I look forward to that." She opened her door and the sound of water lapping echoed.

Lake Ponchartrain.

It made perfect sense.

They'd discussed coming here to talk after the photo shoot, for time alone together, to build on their relationship. Now she was fulfilling that plan that had been cut short.

His door opened and she pulled off his blindfold. Sure enough, Gabrielle stood silhouetted by the lake, the setting sun casting tequila-colored warmth over her face.

He joined her, holding his hand out for hers, clasping in a perfect fit. The blindfold she'd used on him—the satin sash from her bathrobe—trailed from her pocket in a floral splash riding the wind. They walked that way for at least ten minutes, reminding him of times past when they'd enjoyed that rare gift of two people able to coexist even in silence.

As the sky grew darker and the city lights flickered to life, Gabrielle's steps slowed, her attention out there somewhere on the lake.

"Hank, my love for you is like that lake, it's powerful and fluid, and a natural force I can't deny any longer." She stopped, facing him, as serious as he'd ever seen her. "I want to be with you forever, here, Bossier City, wherever that love takes us around the world."

Her declaration was even more than he could have hoped for and almost sent him to his knees. He clasped her shoulders and put his all in what he'd been waiting two years to tell her. He wouldn't botch it this time.

"Gabrielle, I've been in love with you since the first time I saw you. But I'm willing to take it one day at a time if that's what you need, because every day with you is better than a lifetime without you."

"Oh, God, Hank, I want it all with you, so much." She cradled his face in her hands and kissed him, fully, openly and with the promise of more to come. "I love you, more than I ever thought it would be possible to love anyone. I don't want to wait. I just want us to be happy together every day for the rest of our lives."

He hauled her close and let the relief shudder through him until he could trust himself to speak again. He buried his face in her hair. "About my job in the military, if it's a deal breaker for you, I'll get out. I've done a lot of soul searching with my dad since you left. He helped me start coming to grips with what happened over there. He's helping me reevaluate a lot of things. I know what's most important to me now."

"Hank," she gasped, arching back. "Didn't you hear me say that I love you, anywhere that takes us? You don't have to give that up for me. I don't want you to do that."

"Wait. Let me finish. Yes, my job is important to me, but you are more important and I'm not willing to lose you over this. I'm lucky. I have financial choices."

She looked right back at him, her steely resolve glimmering in the hazy sunset. "I love you too much to ask you to give up something that's so much a part of who you are. All I ask is that we're partners, that we keep working at making our relationship stronger. And that we get a permanent home when you retire."

She appeared to mean what she said, but he wasn't risking his future with her by just grasping her offer without careful consideration. "How about we take it a day at a time with the military-life decision? If you change your mind, tell me. I may have followed my dad's career path in some ways, but I have no dreams of being a general."

"But you could be," she insisted with a faith in him that he appreciated.

"I have plans for a business I would like to start, a spin-off with my computer partner. I was thinking New Orleans would make a good home base. In fact—if you agree—I would like to get a head start on that home by buying the Garden District house we've been renting. We'll have roots here, whether I stay in the air force or not."

Happiness and peace spread across her face. "I can live with that plan as long as I'm living with you."

"And about our big, pushy families?" His thumb stroked along her neck, taking note of her speeding pulse and silky skin. "If we decide to invite them into our lives more often?"

"I think we're lucky to have them," she said without hesitation. "Beyond the fact that they're actually pretty amazing people, they're also very eager to babysit."

His imagination sparked with how they could fill their time alone in a deserted stretch of moonlit water. "Are you propositioning me?"

She pulled the blindfold from her jeans pocket. "I have some plans of my own, if you're game."

He spread his arms wide. "I'm all yours."

Epilogue

New Orleans: A Year Later

"Laissez les bons temps rouler!" Let the good times roll!

The cheer bounced around inside Gabrielle Ballard Renshaw's head as she pushed through the Mardi Gras crowd lining the road to watch the informal neighborhood parade pass her house. Her mood was totally party-worthy. But she needed to deliver a message to Hank, a very personal message. Tracking down her boyfriend— her husband of two months—lit her soul.

Excitement powered her forward, one step at a time through the throng of partiers decked out in jester hats, masks and beads. Lampposts blazed through the dark. The parade inched past, a jazz band blasting a Louis Armstrong number while necklaces, doubloons and even candy rained over the mini-mob, that also happened to be all family gathered on her front lawn. It wasn't the official parade, but a smaller one put together in conjunction with a local fundraiser.

She loved this town she now considered her home base, somewhere to come back to no matter where they were stationed.

The past year had been hectic and blissful as she and Hank figured out ways to blend their lives while she completed her degree this past Christmas. She thumbed her diamond solitaire and diamond-studded wedding band, in a simple style they'd chosen together. Her scrapbooking skills were getting a workout recording all the amazing memories.

They'd been married just after the holidays in a simple wedding, only family at the base chapel. Hank had worn his formal uniform and they'd carried Max down the aisle with them. Their one claim to pageantry had been a B-52 fly-over as they'd walked out the chapel doors as man and wife.

Although she did move up to Bossier City with him and he'd stayed in the air force, she'd insisted on keeping some of her business contacts. In a surprise twist during their Christmas gathering of all the relatives at the family compound, Gabrielle had found herself brainstorming with Hank's older brother—the lawyer who oversaw the Landis/Renshaw Foundation. Before the pumpkin pie had been sliced, they'd pulled together ideas for starting a scholarship to benefit children of military veterans who'd died in the line of duty. The funds would be awarded in Kevin's name.

Peace didn't arrive in a single day. But she and Hank were building a future together while still acknowledging a dear man who'd been such an integral part of both their lives. Another gift from Kevin, they no longer isolated themselves. They'd learned to embrace and appreciate their families while building their own life together.

Her eyes tracked to her precious, *healthy* son playing with his cousins under a sprawling oak with twinkling lights in Mardi Gras colors of green, purple and gold. Wearing his pj's, he ran in high-speed circles with his cousins, all under Leonie's watchful eye. She served as the caretaker for their Garden District house when they were away, and helped with nanny duties during visits.

Finally, Gabrielle made her way past their huge extended family to her husband. Hank caught her eye and peeled away from their male relatives all giving input on how to tie a piñata from the tree.

His strong and steady arms went around her waist, pulling her as close as was appropriate around so many watchful eyes. "Hello, Mrs. Renshaw."

"And hello to you, Major." She toyed with the buttons on his chambray shirt.

"What did the doctor say? And you'd better talk fast because it's killing me that I didn't get to go with you."

She'd made an appointment to see her old doctor while they were in town for Mardi Gras. Hank had wanted to meet her there, but she'd insisted he stay with the family. She'd been almost afraid to hope and wanted to keep the appointment low key.

Wow, had she been in for a pleasant surprise.

Who knew that contentment and excitement could co-exist? "This family has more than we expected to celebrate tonight, because, yes, I'm seven weeks pregnant. It happened on our honeymoon."

"And you're happy?"

"I'm ecstatic! And you?" Although she could already see the answer in his electric-blue eyes, lighting from inside.

He cradled her face in large tender hands. "Max is going to love his little sister."

"It could be a boy." She leaned closer, her back foot lifting.

"But it's a girl," he said without hesitation.

"You're a pushy guy, you know that?"

"Thank goodness I found a woman strong enough to stand beside me for life."

And their life together was better than she'd ever dreamed, thanks to her mother's help in realizing she didn't have to be a wonder woman. Doing her best and accepting the best from others bonded them all into a beautiful family.

"Celebrate with me soon?" she whispered against his mouth.

"Celebrate now." He spun her around as the parade marched past. *"Laissez les bons temps rouler,* my love. Let the good times roll."

* * * * *

PASSION

COMING NEXT MONTH
AVAILABLE MAY 8, 2012

#2155 UNDONE BY HER TENDER TOUCH
Pregnancy & Passion
Maya Banks
When one night with magnate Cam Hollingsworth results in pregnancy, no-strings-attached turns into a tangled web for caterer Pippa Laingley.

#2156 ONE DANCE WITH THE SHEIKH
Dynasties: The Kincaids
Tessa Radley

#2157 THE TIES THAT BIND
Billionaires and Babies
Emilie Rose

#2158 AN INTIMATE BARGAIN
Colorado Cattle Barons
Barbara Dunlop

#2159 RELENTLESS PURSUIT
Lone Star Legacy
Sara Orwig

#2160 READY FOR HER CLOSE-UP
Matchmakers, Inc.
Katherine Garbera

HDCNM0412

REQUEST YOUR FREE BOOKS!

2 FREE NOVELS PLUS 2 FREE GIFTS!

Harlequin

Desire

ALWAYS POWERFUL, PASSIONATE AND PROVOCATIVE

YES! Please send me 2 FREE Harlequin Desire® novels and my 2 FREE gifts (gifts are worth about $10). After receiving them, if I don't wish to receive any more books, I can return the shipping statement marked "cancel." If I don't cancel, I will receive 6 brand-new novels every month and be billed just $4.30 per book in the U.S. or $4.99 per book in Canada. That's a saving of at least 14% off the cover price! It's quite a bargain! Shipping and handling is just 50¢ per book in the U.S. and 75¢ per book in Canada.* I understand that accepting the 2 free books and gifts places me under no obligation to buy anything. I can always return a shipment and cancel at any time. Even if I never buy another book, the two free books and gifts are mine to keep forever.

225/326 HDN FEF3

Name _____ (PLEASE PRINT)

Address _____ Apt. #

City _____ State/Prov. _____ Zip/Postal Code

Signature (if under 18, a parent or guardian must sign)

Mail to the **Reader Service:**

IN U.S.A.: P.O. Box 1867, Buffalo, NY 14240-1867
IN CANADA: P.O. Box 609, Fort Erie, Ontario L2A 5X3

Not valid for current subscribers to Harlequin Desire books.

Want to try two free books from another line?
Call 1-800-873-8635 or visit www.ReaderService.com.

* Terms and prices subject to change without notice. Prices do not include applicable taxes. Sales tax applicable in N.Y. Canadian residents will be charged applicable taxes. Offer not valid in Quebec. This offer is limited to one order per household. All orders subject to credit approval. Credit or debit balances in a customer's account(s) may be offset by any other outstanding balance owed by or to the customer. Please allow 4 to 6 weeks for delivery. Offer available while quantities last.

Your Privacy—The Reader Service is committed to protecting your privacy. Our Privacy Policy is available online at www.ReaderService.com or upon request from the Reader Service.

We make a portion of our mailing list available to reputable third parties that offer products we believe may interest you. If you prefer that we not exchange your name with third parties, or if you wish to clarify or modify your communication preferences, please visit us at www.ReaderService.com/consumerchoice or write to us at Reader Service Preference Service, P.O. Box 9062, Buffalo, NY 14269. Include your complete name and address.

HDES11B

"**W**ould you like some help?"

Pippa whirled around, still holding the bottle of champagne, and darn near tossed the contents onto the floor.

"Help?"

Cam nodded slowly. "Assistance? You look as though you could use it. How on earth did you think you'd manage to cater this event on your own?"

Pippa was horrified by his offer and then, as she processed the rest of his statement, she was irritated as hell.

"I'd hate for you to sully those pretty hands," she snapped. "And for your information, I've got this under control. The help didn't show. Not my fault. The food is impeccable, if I do say so myself. I just need to deliver it to the guests."

"I believe I just offered my assistance and you insulted me," Cam said dryly.

Her eyebrows drew together. Oh, why did the man have to be so damn delicious-looking? And why could she never perform the simplest functions around him?

"You're Ashley's guest," Pippa said firmly. "Not to mention you're used to being served, not serving others."

"How do you know what I'm used to?" he asked mildly.

She had absolutely nothing to say to that and watched in bewilderment as he hefted the tray up and walked out of the kitchen.

She sagged against the sink, her pulse racing hard enough

to make her dizzy.

Cameron Hollingsworth was gorgeous, unpolished in a rough and totally sexy way, arrogant and so wrong for her. But there was something about the man that just did it for her.

She sighed. He was a luscious specimen of a male and he couldn't be any less interested in her.

Even so, she was itching to shake his world up a little.

Realizing she was spending far too much time mooning over Cameron, she grabbed another tray, took a deep breath to compose herself and then headed toward the living room.

And Cameron Hollingsworth.

Will Pippa shake up Cameron's world?
Find out in Maya Banks's passionate new novel

UNDONE BY HER TENDER TOUCH

Available May 2012 from Harlequin® Desire!

Royalty has never been so scandalous!

When Crown Prince Alessandro of Santina proposes
to paparazzi favorite Allegra Jackson it promises
to be *the* social event of the decade!

Harlequin Presents® invites you to step into the decadent
playground of the world's rich and famous and rub shoulders
with royalty, sheikhs and glamorous socialites.

Collect all 8 passionate tales written by *USA TODAY* bestselling authors, beginning May 2012!